She had expe
stranger, fore
had intervened, but to her utter
astonishment the man looking
back at her was someone she
knew.

Intimately.

She hadn't seen him in four long years, but his face was so achingly familiar that she suddenly felt her legs weaken, thinking for a moment that she might collapse again.

All at once her heart began to thump wildly against her chest and she couldn't quite breathe as shock began to overcome her.

He smiled at her then, a smile laced with a hint of melancholy, a subtle sadness reflected in his intense blue eyes—eyes that spoke of a history between them that would never be forgotten.

"How've you been, Anna?"

The man she had once hoped to marry.

ALANA MATTHEWS

BODY ARMOR

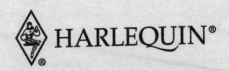

HARLEQUIN®

TORONTO • NEW YORK • LONDON
AMSTERDAM • PARIS • SYDNEY • HAMBURG
STOCKHOLM • ATHENS • TOKYO • MILAN • MADRID
PRAGUE • WARSAW • BUDAPEST • AUCKLAND

If you purchased this book without a cover you should be aware that this book is stolen property. It was reported as "unsold and destroyed" to the publisher, and neither the author nor the publisher has received any payment for this "stripped book."

Recycling programs for this product may not exist in your area.

ISBN-13: 978-0-373-69506-5

BODY ARMOR

Copyright © 2010 by Alana Matthews

All rights reserved. Except for use in any review, the reproduction or utilization of this work in whole or in part in any form by any electronic, mechanical or other means, now known or hereafter invented, including xerography, photocopying and recording, or in any information storage or retrieval system, is forbidden without the written permission of the publisher, Harlequin Enterprises Limited, 225 Duncan Mill Road, Don Mills, Ontario M3B 3K9, Canada.

This is a work of fiction. Names, characters, places and incidents are either the product of the author's imagination or are used fictitiously, and any resemblance to actual persons, living or dead, business establishments, events or locales is entirely coincidental.

This edition published by arrangement with Harlequin Books S.A.

For questions and comments about the quality of this book please contact us at Customer_eCare@Harlequin.ca.

® and TM are trademarks of the publisher. Trademarks indicated with ® are registered in the United States Patent and Trademark Office, the Canadian Trade Marks Office and in other countries.

www.eHarlequin.com

Printed in U.S.A.

ABOUT THE AUTHOR

Alana Matthews can't remember a time when she didn't want to be a writer. As a child, she was a permanent fixture in her local library, and soon turned her passion for books into writing short stories and finally novels. A longtime fan of romantic suspense, Alana felt she had no choice but to try her hand at the genre, and she is thrilled to be writing for Harlequin Intrigue. Alana makes her home in a small town near the coast of Southern California, where she spends her time writing, composing music and watching her favorite movies.

Send a message to Alana at her website, www.AlanaMatthews.com.

Books by Alana Matthews

HARLEQUIN INTRIGUE
1208—MAN UNDERCOVER
1239—BODY ARMOR

Don't miss any of our special offers. Write to us at the following address for information on our newest releases.

Harlequin Reader Service
U.S.: 3010 Walden Ave., P.O. Box 1325, Buffalo, NY 14269
Canadian: P.O. Box 609, Fort Erie, Ont. L2A 5X3

CAST OF CHARACTERS

Anna Sanford—The recent death of her brother has been ruled a suicide, but Anna doesn't believe it.

Brody Carpenter—Once a sheriff's deputy accused of taking a bribe, Brody will always regret walking away four years ago. Now tragedy has brought him back home.

Adam—Anna's three-year-old son and her reason for living.

Deputy Frank Matson—He tried to pick up the pieces when Brody left, but still couldn't repair the damage.

Joe Wilson—Frank's partner, whose dislike for Brody Carpenter knows no bounds.

Sylvia Sanderson—Anna's grieving mother once welcomed Brody into their home. Now she wishes he'd go away.

Sakey and Chercover—Two thugs who want something from Anna that she doesn't know she has.

Owen Sanderson—His sudden suicide has raised Anna's suspicions. The message he sent just before his death brought Brody home.

Chapter One

There was something not quite right about Santa Claus.

Anna didn't *see* it so much as *feel* it, a vague uneasiness that spread through her the moment he glanced in her direction. But it was there, and it was unmistakable, and she wondered for a moment if she should call security and have him checked out.

He stood in the middle of the crowded mall, between Anna's shop and a small dress boutique across the aisle, ringing his bell next to a Save the Children donation canister. Something in his eyes said he couldn't care less about the children, however, and for the brief moment he looked at Anna, she was pretty sure his interest lay somewhere else entirely.

Like the area just south of her neck and shoulders.

Anna was in the middle of helping a customer—a gentle old woman who wanted a peach-blossom body care set for her granddaughter—and did her best to ignore Santa's leer, chalking it up to typical

Neanderthal behavior. But Anna had her share of lascivious looks in the past, and this one seemed to go beyond the norm and straight into the realm of creepy.

Was this guy even authorized to be here?

He wasn't your typical holiday bell ringer. Most were retirees looking for something to do, but not this one.

He was about thirty years old, and there was a shady, wanted-poster quality to his demeanor that couldn't be disguised by the floppy hat and the fake white beard. Strip away the red suit and all the padding, and you'd probably find a common street thug underneath.

Maybe Anna wasn't being very charitable herself. Maybe he was just a poor unfortunate who was down on his luck and needed any job he could find. That wasn't unusual in this economy.

After what she'd been through over the past week, Anna would be the first to admit she wasn't in the greatest frame of mind. So maybe she should cut this guy a break.

Still, there was a sense of menace in his look that seemed to say he *wanted* something from her, and the kernel of dread doing somersaults through her stomach right now was not a feeling she could easily ignore.

Just go away, she felt like telling him. *Pack up your stuff and leave.*

And to her surprise, a few minutes later, he did.

ANNA HAD DOUBTS ABOUT coming back to work tonight. Thought it might be too soon. In fact, she didn't normally *work* at night, but with only three days left until Christmas, and a store overflowing with anxious last-minute shoppers, she didn't feel she had a choice.

Trudy had done a wonderful job of covering for her the past week, but it was time for Anna to swallow her grief and get on with her life. If not for herself, then for little Adam. He deserved a normal Christmas.

As normal as it could be, that is.

She also had other matters to consider. Anna's Body Essentials was *her* baby, and with her lease about to expire and her rental fee threatening to increase, she couldn't afford to sit at home obsessing over all the things she could have said or done that might have kept her brother, Owen, alive.

The sheriff's department psychologist had told her that it's typical for the family of suicides to wonder where they might have gone wrong.

"Owen took his life because he *wanted* to," he'd said somberly. "Not because anyone drove him to it. It's unlikely there's any way you could have stopped him, short of catching him in the act."

"My mother thinks that if we'd paid more attention, seen the signs…"

"The signs aren't always evident, Anna. Especially when you only see someone a couple times a week.

Owen probably felt it was his duty to put on a brave face, make everyone believe he was okay. Such behavior isn't atypical."

Anna had listened carefully, nodding politely, more stunned by this turn of events than the psychologist could ever possibly know, but she hadn't said what she was thinking at the time.

That she wasn't entirely convinced that Owen *had* committed suicide.

It just didn't make sense.

Admittedly, her brother had seemed agitated lately, and he hadn't been in the best frame of mind after losing his job. But he was one of the most happy-go-lucky people Anna had ever known, and even if he *was* depressed, she just couldn't believe he'd try to find the solution through a bullet to the head.

Not the Owen Sanford she knew.

She had no proof of this, of course. Just gut instinct. But one thing Anna had learned in her time on this planet was that her instincts were rarely wrong.

When she finally broke down and confessed this belief to the psychologist, however, she was treated as if she were a child with a vivid imagination, her ability to reason clouded by grief.

And who knows? Maybe that was true.

Maybe she hadn't known Owen as well as she thought she had.

AFTER SAYING GOOD-NIGHT to her last customer around 11:00 p.m., Anna closed up shop then spent another hour in her office, catching up on some of the bookkeeping she'd neglected for the past week. As she worked, her gaze drifted to a photo of her brother on the desktop, the one with that smile that always reminded her of their father.

She remembered how strong Owen had been when Daddy had his heart attack. How he had stepped up and become a man in the face of their tragedy, consoling their devastated mother and watching after an eleven-year-old sister who had handled her grief badly by withdrawing from the world, locked in her room, blasting Nirvana at all hours.

That girl was all grown up now, with a three-year-old son and a two-year-old divorce, doing her best to eke out a living as she coped with yet another family tragedy. And the sad irony was that the person she needed most right now was Owen.

Little Adam needed him, too. After the divorce, Owen had taken over as surrogate father, and she knew that his absence in her son's life was a hole about the size of Veterans Memorial Stadium.

A hole that might never be filled.

Anna felt tears in her eyes and knew that this was her cue. She couldn't pretend anymore. She was just going through the motions here and needed to get home.

Shutting down her computer, she grabbed her keys

and her purse and her jacket and let herself out the back door.

Then she navigated the wide hallway to the service elevator, still thinking about Owen and trying very hard not to cry.

THE UNDERGROUND PARKING lot was nearly empty at this hour.

There were maybe five cars total, most of them hidden by shadow. The maintenance down here was shoddy at best and half the fluorescent bulbs were either dead or on life support. It was the *employees* lot, after all, and who cared about the employees?

Anna was almost to her car, a gray Ford sedan, her footsteps reverberating against the cement walls, when she thought she saw a flicker of movement in the corner of her eye.

She paused, turned, found nothing there. But that didn't keep her heartbeat from kicking up a notch.

Was she alone?

Feeling the sudden need to move quickly, she continued on toward her car, fumbling for her keys as she went, pressing the remote to unlock it. A moment later she was at the door, about to open it, thinking she was just being silly and paranoid, when—

—wham—

—a pair of hands grabbed her from behind, pushing her back toward the aisle. Headlights came alive in a dark corner and a battered green van shot toward her.

Anna tried to twist away. Saw that her attacker was none other than *Santa Claus,* still wearing that ridiculous hat and white beard—his face hard, his eyes as empty as the parking lot—and she knew immediately that she was in *very big trouble.*

"Where is it?" he hissed. "Where's the button?"

This surprised Anna. She had no earthly idea what he was talking about. She sputtered something unintelligible, the dread she'd felt earlier coming back like a blow to the belly.

She tried again to twist away, but he kept shoving her into the aisle.

"We know he gave it to you—*where is it?*"

He shoved her hard and she slammed against the side of the van, which was directly in front of them now. Reaching out, he gripped a handle, slid the door open then grabbed her again and pushed her toward the seats inside.

"Get in."

"Please," she cried, "I don't understand what you want from me."

"The hell you don't." Anna heard a soft *snick.* Santa had popped his switchblade. He pointed it at her throat. "Get in, sugar lips, or I'll cut you right—"

There was a roar behind them—a rumbling, beefy engine coming to life, filling the parking lot with the sound of a jet taking off.

They both turned and saw a large black motorcycle emerge from the shadows. It rocketed straight toward them and didn't slow down, the driver's face hidden by his helmet and visor.

Santa's eyes went wide and he grabbed Anna by her jacket and spun her around, pushing her directly into the bike's path.

Then he was scrambling into the van, shouting "Go! Go! Go!" as Anna stumbled forward and lost her footing, falling to her knees.

Pain shot through her as her kneecaps pounded into the asphalt. The bike roared straight for her, its lone headlight illuminating her terrified face. Then it quickly veered to the right, its driver laying the machine on its side as he struggled to maintain some kind of control.

The bike skidded into a cement post, crashing to an abrupt halt, but the rider had already jumped free and rolled to his feet. He pulled a gun from the small of his back as he started running toward the van.

The van peeled out, laying a long patch of rubber, the squeal so loud it pierced Anna's eardrums like feedback, as the man in the motorcycle helmet raised his gun.

But before he could fire, the van screeched around a corner and up the exit ramp, disappearing from sight.

The man in the helmet looked as if he might squeeze off a shot anyway, but then he lowered the gun, tucked it under his leather jacket and turned toward Anna.

Seeing that she was still on her knees, he moved quickly and helped her to her feet.

"Are you all right?"

Anna nodded, wincing against the pain, and looked up at him as he reached for the visor and raised it.

She had expected to see a stranger, forever grateful that he had intervened, but to her utter astonishment the man looking back at her was someone she knew.

Intimately.

She hadn't seen him in four long years, but it was a face so achingly familiar that she suddenly felt her legs weaken, thinking for a moment that she might collapse again.

All at once her heart began to thump wildly against her chest and she couldn't quite breathe as shock began to overcome her.

He smiled at her then, a smile laced with a hint of melancholy, a subtle sadness reflected in his intense blue eyes—eyes that spoke of a history between them that would never be forgotten.

"How've you been, Anna?"

It was Brody Carpenter.

Owen's best friend.

The man she had once hoped to marry.

Chapter Two

Anna didn't know where even to begin.

After all these years she had pretty much given up on ever seeing Brody again. Had halfway convinced herself that he was either dead or living under an alias somewhere, never to be found.

Her life with him seemed to be part of some vague, half-imagined fantasy relegated to a part of her mind she rarely visited. Surely no more than once or twice a day.

Yet here he stood in front of her. Not an illusion, but a living, breathing human being who didn't look much different from how she remembered him. The same rugged jawline, the same hard, angular body. The wide shoulders. The strong hands. Towering over her as he always had.

She suddenly felt as if she'd been hurtled into the past—a feeling that was both exhilarating and unsettling. She couldn't decide whether to slap him across the face or throw her arms around him and hug him as if he were a soldier who had just returned home from the war.

In the end, she did neither.

Brody Carpenter. A name that had sent shivers of pleasure through her ever since the day she first met him, nearly fifteen years ago. A name he had once promised to share with her.

Before he broke her heart.

Anna tried to speak, but she could barely put together a sentence. "What… What are you doing here?"

"Saving your life, I think. Those idiots looked like they meant business."

"I mean what are you doing in Cedarwood? We all thought you were—"

"Dead?"

She nodded. Then shook her head. "No. No, I never really thought that."

"I wouldn't blame you if you did," he said.

Anna stared at him. "It's just you disappeared so suddenly after the trial, and every time we tried to contact you, you'd either changed your number or moved on, and…"

She couldn't finish. The thought was too exhausting. Too painful. All the heartbreak she'd felt back then was bubbling up to the surface, compounding the grief she'd been battling ever since Owen died.

Then she realized that this was why Brody was here.

He'd heard about Owen.

Somehow word had gotten to him that his best friend since high school, the boy who had played wide receiver to his quarterback, had taken his own life.

But before she could ask him about this, a door near the service elevator boomed open.

"Hands! Show us your hands!"

Two security guards stood near the stairwell, out of breath, their weapons leveled directly at Brody.

He slowly raised his hands to show them empty. "Easy, boys. Take it easy."

"Don't move," one of the guards warned.

Anna knew him. Barely out of his teens, he looked as nervous as a kid facing off against a gang of bullies, and she was afraid he might get stupid and actually pull the trigger.

"You okay, Ms. Sanford? We saw him grab you on the surveillance cameras. The sheriff's on the way."

"He's not the one you're after," Anna said. "Put your guns down or somebody might get hurt."

The kid considered this, glancing at Brody's fallen motorcycle before returning his gaze to Anna. "You sure you're okay?"

"Still in one piece, thanks to him."

The guard spent a long moment evaluating the situation then finally holstered his gun. His partner followed suit.

Relieved, Anna released a long, shaky breath.
"Thank you," she said.

WHEN THE SHERIFF'S patrol car glided into the lot,
the young guard crossed toward it, waving his hands
to let the deputies know that everything was under
control.

The car came to a stop in the middle of the aisle.
As the deputies climbed out, one of them took a look
at Brody, his eyes lighting up in surprise and de-
light.

"Carpenter? Is that you?"

"That's the rumor," Brody said then shook the
deputy's hand. "Good to see you, Brett."

Anna wasn't surprised that they knew each other.
Before dropping off the face of the earth, Brody Carpenter had been one of Cedarwood, Iowa's finest
sheriff's deputies. A man destined for great things.

Until it all went seriously wrong.

"Man, we all figured you were dead," the deputy
said. "Where the heck you been for the past four
years?"

"It would probably take that long to explain,"
Brody told him.

"Can't say I blame you for disappearing like you
did. Brass did everything they could to make an ex-
ample of you. Scared the heck out of all of us."

Anna had no doubt that Brody still had a lot friends
in the department, many of whom knew—just as she

had—that he'd gotten a raw deal. He'd been accused of destroying evidence against a local drug kingpin and taking a payoff for the effort.

The county undersheriff had forced him to resign long before the case against him had been fully evaluated, and despite his eventual acquittal, Anna knew that Brody had considered it a matter that should never have come to trial. There were people on the force who were working against him, he'd told her, trying to destroy the dream he'd carried with him since he was a boy.

And they had succeeded. Their cynicism and petty politics ultimately won, even if the prosecutor hadn't. Rather than reinstate Brody to a job that he more than deserved—a job he had earned and excelled at—his bosses had turned their backs on him. Proclaimed him guilty despite what the jury had decided.

He was a tarnished warrior, and Anna knew better than anyone that the entire ordeal had deeply wounded him. She'd felt his pain more than even *he* could know.

But that wasn't an excuse to run away. To abandon your friends and the woman you love. And as relieved as she was to see him, to know that he was safe, she wasn't sure she'd ever be able to forgive him.

Where *had* he been for the past four years?

And why hadn't *she* been with him?

As Brody and the deputy dredged up old memories, he glanced at her and she once again felt her heart stutter, a feeling she'd never been able to control. His look was so full of regret that it took everything she had to keep from crying.

She wanted to punch him, kiss him, scream at him, make love to him, tell him to go back to wherever he came from and stay there—all at the same time.

She didn't need this now. Couldn't handle it. She was normally a strong woman, but at that moment the world seemed to be caving in on her—Owen, the attack, now Brody—and she began to wonder about her capacity to stay upright. She felt dizzy and her vision seemed to narrow.

"I have to sit down," she said suddenly, and before the words were fully out of her mouth, Brody took her by the arm, helping her to the asphalt as the others crowded around her to see if she was okay.

"I'm fine," she told them. "I'll be all right. I just feel a little faint."

As if this was the kick in the butt they needed, the deputies now got down to business, Brett pulling a notepad out of his back pocket and asking Brody to give him a run-through of the incident.

The other deputy took the two guards aside to question them, as well.

Anna listened as Brody explained that he'd seen her get off the elevator and head for her car, when a guy in a Santa suit popped up out of nowhere and grabbed her. Then instinct kicked in and Brody did what had to be done.

"I just wish they hadn't gotten away," he said.

"Did you get a tag number?"

Brody shook his head. "I'm a little out of practice. And everything happened so fast."

"I'm curious," the deputy said. "Why were you even down here? Was Anna expecting you?"

Brody glanced at her again. He seemed a bit thrown by the question, but he recovered quickly.

"I was waiting for her. Hoping to get the chance to talk to her. About Owen."

"Owen?"

"My brother," Anna explained. "He died a few days ago."

"I'm sorry to hear that. My condolences." He looked from one to the other. "So this guy in the Santa Claus suit. Do either of you have any idea who he is?"

They both shook their heads. "Not a clue," said. "But he seemed to want something from me. Kept asking me about a button."

"Button? What kind of button?"

"I have no idea. I don't know what he was talking about."

"What about the driver? Either of you get a look at him?"

Again they shook their heads.

"Well, we'll take a gander at the surveillance footage. Hopefully we'll find something useful, but with this lousy lighting down here, I'm not counting on it." He turned to Anna. "Can you think of anyone who would want to harm you?"

Anna didn't have to think. The answer was a resounding *no*. Her life was wrapped up in the shop and Adam, and her potential to make enemies was, at best, slim. She had absolutely no idea why Santa had grabbed her.

She remembered the creepy leer he'd given her as he rang that bell outside her shop, but she never thought it would come to this.

She suddenly wondered if he'd been stalking her. And that put a whole new spin on things.

She'd been scared before, but now she was petrified.

What if he came back?

She told them about the earlier encounter, and the deputy assured her that they'd be speaking to mall management to find out if anyone could identify the guy.

"I'd like to be in on that," Brody said. "Get a look at the surveillance footage myself."

The deputy hesitated. "I'm sure we'll have video for you, but you're a witness, Brody—you know we can't let you get involved in the investigation. Besides, it isn't really up to me. I'm just the responding deputy."

"But you'll keep us apprised?"

Us? Anna thought. Was there suddenly an *us* now?

The presumption annoyed her. Did Brody think that he could show up out of the blue and immediately resume where they'd left off?

There *was* no us as far as she was concerned. Despite her mixed emotions, she at least knew that much. And at that moment she realized just how angry with him she really was. Even if he *had* saved her life.

Her light-headedness abruptly gone, she pushed herself off the asphalt and stood. As Brody moved to help her, she shifted away from him.

"I'm fine," she said curtly, and she could see by his reaction that he was both startled and hurt.

But she didn't care. His hurt couldn't possibly compare to what she'd gone through after he left.

The deputy, sensing the tension between them, said, "I think that's enough questions from me, but we got a call on the way in that a detective is already headed to the scene. I'm sure he'll have a few of his own."

As if on cue, a sleek white sedan turned a corner and rolled down the aisle toward them.

"Speak of the devil."

As the sedan drew closer, Anna saw the driver and thought for a moment that her head might just explode.

Could this night get any more complicated?

Whatever gods were conspiring against her, they

must have been mightily amused. She couldn't quite believe who had been dispatched to the scene, and she was convinced that it was no accident.

Despite its size, Cedarwood, Iowa, was starting to feel like a very small town.

The sedan came to a stop, then the engine shut down and two plainclothes sheriff's detectives climbed out, the driver buttoning his suit coat as he sauntered toward them, a look of concern on his face.

"You all right, babe?"

Hail, hail, the gang's all here, Anna thought.

It was her ex-husband, Frank.

Chapter Three

When the two detectives stepped out of the cruiser, Brody felt his whole body go stiff. The last thing he needed right now was an encounter with Frank Matson.

While he'd known that coming back to Cedarwood would dredge up a lot of old emotions and hostilities, he hadn't expected it all to happen in one night. He marveled at how cruel fate could sometimes be, and he knew that Anna was probably feeling it, too.

Matson's concentration centered on her, genuine concern in his eyes. "You all right, babe?"

It took him a moment to finally look at Brody, and when he did, the world seemed to stop for a moment as the reality of what he'd just walked into began to sink in.

"Carpenter?"

"The one and only," Brody said. "How you been, Frank?"

Matson's concern abruptly vanished, replaced by a hardness that betrayed his utter contempt for Brody.

They had been rivals since high school—rivals for Anna's heart, to be precise—and Brody had a hard time reconciling the fact that Anna had not only been married to the man but given birth to his child.

But then a lot had happened in his absence.

And whose fault was that?

Matson frowned at him. "What are you doing here, Carpenter? Are you part of this?"

"Meaning what?"

Matson moved in close. "Meaning if you've done anything to hurt Anna…"

Brody didn't back away. "You see any cuffs on me?"

"Oh, for God's sakes," Anna said. "Both of you, stop it. You don't see each other in years and you just pick up where you left off?"

Matson backed down first. "Sorry, babe, you're right."

"Quit calling me that."

He threw his hands up. "All right, all right. You're upset, I understand. But I hear over the radio that someone at the mall has been attacked and the name Sanford comes up, you might understand why *I'm* a little upset, too. Did they hurt you?"

"No. Thanks to Brody."

Matson shifted his gaze again. "Your knight in shining armor. I guess things never really change."

Brody felt heat rising in his chest. "Look, Frank, I've got no beef with you. Do we need to make an unpleasant situation even worse? If you care about Anna—"

"If *I* care about her?" His eyebrows went up. "I'm the one who picked up the pieces when you left her behind, hotshot. And I don't know if you remember, but I supported you. Told the undersheriff that Internal Affairs had the wrong guy." He shook his head in disgust. "That support stopped the minute you ran out on Anna."

Brody said nothing. There wasn't much he *could* say. Matson was right. He could try to explain that he'd been in a strange place at the time, that he hadn't been thinking straight and just needed to get away from Cedarwood and all the whispers. People thinking he was dirty and had just gotten lucky.

But Matson had never been the kind of guy who would understand such things. He had one switch: on and off. And if you didn't conform to his narrow view of the world, you were the object of his derision.

And maybe Brody deserved that.

"Look," he said. "I don't want to argue with you."

"Of course you don't. Things get too hot for Brody Carpenter, he'll hop on his little motor scooter and run for the—"

"*Stop!*" Anna said.

She turned away, moving across the aisle toward her car, and Matson immediately followed her, stopping her before she reached it. Brody watched as he took her aside, trying to console her, calm her down. He could plainly see that Matson still cared for her.

Brody didn't know what had gone wrong between them, but it was clear that Frank wasn't over it yet. Not by a long shot.

Who could blame him? Anna wasn't the type of woman you get over.

Brody never had.

But he was the outsider here. The intruder. And despite their differences, he could see that she was in good hands with Matson. Maybe he should just back off and let the department do what it did best.

For now, at least.

Moving to his Harley, he lifted it off the asphalt and checked it for damage—some scrapes and dings. He'd pulled it out of storage three days ago and was surprised to discover how much he'd missed riding it.

He approached his old buddy Brett, who was huddled in conversation with Frank's partner, Joe Wilson. Wilson's contempt for him seemed even deeper than Frank's.

"Why are you here, Carpenter?"

"Just doing a friend a favor. You think I can cut out now? I already gave Brett my statement."

Wilson narrowed his eyes at him. "Guards tell us you used a piece tonight. You still got a carry permit?"

Brody nodded. "I'm up-to-date. Not sure why I kept renewing it, but I did."

"Yeah, well you better believe we'll be checking into that. You staying some place we can reach you?"

"The Motor Court Inn. On Sycamore."

"Get out of here," Wilson said. "Can't stand the sight of you anyway."

Brody let the comment pass. He nodded to Brett then climbed on his bike and started it up. The thunderous roar filled the parking lot, getting Anna and Matson's attention. Anna looked at him expectantly.

Their gazes connected, but Brody couldn't read her as he used to.

She was still as beautiful as ever, and he'd been a fool to leave her behind. A selfish, unthinking fool. Seeing her like this only drove that point home. There were no words, no deeds, that could make up for what he'd done to her. No path to redemption.

He deserved her scorn. Matson's, too.

Grabbing the throttle, he gave them a nod then roared out of the parking lot. That look in Anna's eyes just about broke his aching heart.

FRANK INSISTED ON taking her home.

Anna was too keyed up to resist, so she gave him the keys to her car and let him drive as Joe Wilson followed in the cruiser.

They were silent for most of the ride, Anna running the night's events through her head over and over again, still vacillating between elation and anger over Brody's sudden reappearance.

As she had watched him ride away tonight, she had wondered if another handful of years would pass before she'd see him again.

She remembered how Brody had hesitated when the deputy asked why he was in the parking lot. He'd mentioned Owen, but Anna got the feeling that there was more to it than that. As if there was a specific purpose for his presence there.

But *what,* exactly?

Owen's funeral had come and gone, and there was nothing anyone could do to bring him back. So why was Brody here?

To torture her?

If so, he was succeeding admirably, and as grateful as she was that he'd saved her life, she'd be in a much better place emotionally if her rescuer had turned out to be a kindhearted stranger.

Frank finally broke the silence. "You okay?"

Anna closed her eyes, almost smiled. An involuntary reaction to an impossible situation. There was no humor behind it at all. "I swear if somebody asks me that one more time tonight, I may scream."

"I'm concerned about you—is that so bad?"

"If you were concerned about me, you'd do what I asked you to do."

He looked at her. "You mean Owen?"

She nodded.

"Come on, babe, we've been over this how many times? I know it's hard, but sooner or later you're going to have to accept the simple fact that your brother killed himself. And the sooner you do, the faster you'll heal."

"I can see you're really broken up about it."

Frank frowned. "Don't do that. You know I liked Owen. The point is, if I thought there was even a shred of evidence that he was the victim of foul play..."

"You'd what?" Anna asked. "Make a notation in a report and file it away somewhere?"

"That isn't fair."

"I'm tired of being fair. And I'm tired of people telling me I'm crazy. Owen would never hurt himself. He wouldn't do that to me, or Mom, or to Adam."

Frank sighed. "I'm not trying to be an insensitive jerk here, Anna, but do you know how many times I've heard people say that? I must do death notifications for a dozen suicides every year, and I can't tell you how many of them end with some family member saying exactly what you just said."

"Fine. But were any of those family members attacked by a guy in a parking lot?"

Frank frowned again. "What's that got to do with it?"

"The guy wanted something from me, Frank."

"Yeah. The same thing every guy since junior high has wanted."

"No. I told you what he said about the button."

"Right. Complete and utter nonsense."

"Is it?"

Frank took his gaze from the road and stared at her. "Isn't it? You think you know what he was talking about?"

Anna shook her head. "I don't have a clue. But that wasn't all of it. He also said, '*I know he gave it to you.*'"

"Meaning what?"

Anna was silent for a moment. This was something that had been quietly working at the periphery of her mind ever since Santa had said it.

"What if this button is something that he thinks Owen gave me? Something that Owen himself was killed for?"

Frank was looking at the road again, but she could see by the subtle hardening of his jaw that he wasn't buying this at all.

Then he said, "Anna, I think you need to consider talking to the sheriff's psychologist again."

"Don't shut me out, Frank. That's the last thing I need right now."

"I'm not shutting you out. I'm trying to help you."

"By telling me I'm certifiable?"

Frank sighed and nudged the wheel, pulling up to the curb in front of Anna's house.

Then he turned to her. "That's not what I'm saying, and you know it. Let's pretend for a moment that you're right about this button thing. Did Owen ever mention it to you?"

Anna thought about it, shook her head.

"Did he ever give you something to keep? To hide for him?"

"No," Anna said. "Nothing."

"You're sure about that?"

"As sure as I can be."

Frank took his hands off the wheel, put one on her shoulder. It was meant to be a gesture of support and reassurance, but Anna was long past being reassured by his touch. If she ever had been.

"Look, babe, I know this whole thing has been tough for you, but you've gotta get your head on straight about your brother. Even if I thought there was foul play, I don't have the authority to reopen his case."

"Why am I not surprised?" She pulled away from him and opened her door. The cold December air filled the car as she held out a hand, palm up. "I'll take my keys now."

Frank ignored the request. "What I *can* do," he said, "is catch the punks who attacked you tonight. And if this button business has anything to do with Owen at all—and I'm not saying it does—I'll try to convince the brass that we need to take another look at his suicide."

This was the first sliver of hope Anna had gotten out of him, and her anger suddenly dissolved. "Is that a promise?"

"Cross my heart and hope to die."

She managed a smile. Genuine this time. "Thank you, Frank."

He shrugged. "You'll always be my girl."

It was a phrase he'd used over and over again during their marriage. One that had turned out to be decidedly untrue, but she didn't feel the need to remind him of that. No point in stirring that particular fire.

He took her keys from the ignition and handed them to her. "I don't think it's anything to worry about, but I'll have a unit patrol the area, to make sure you guys are safe."

She nodded her thanks and was about to climb out when she had a sudden thought. "Adam's asleep, but I bet he'd be happy to wake up long enough to say good-night. You want to come up for a minute?"

Frank's expression darkened. "It's late and I need to get home. Maybe some other time."

Then they were out of the car, Frank moving to his cruiser to join Joe. She watched them drive away, wondering how much more emotional turmoil she could go through before she collapsed under the weight of it all.

Collapsing wasn't an option, however. She needed to be strong for Adam. To follow up on her promise to herself and make this as normal a Christmas as she possibly could.

So far that wasn't working out too well.

Maybe life would look a little brighter tomorrow.

MOM WAS ASLEEP ON THE sofa, the TV tuned to a shopping channel. The woman on-screen was hawking a bath and body set that Anna sold for nearly twice the price in her shop. Between the internet and these discount shows, it was a wonder she could make a living at all. Maybe she should join the modern age, open a website and throw customer service out the window.

Anna took off her jacket and hung it on the coat stand. Grabbing a blanket from the pile next to the armchair, she laid it over her mother then gently kissed her forehead. She didn't want to wake her. Mom had been having a rough time of it, too, and sleep was therapeutic.

After turning off the TV, she went upstairs to check in on Adam. His night-light was on, and he was curled up into a tight little ball atop his bed, hugging the toy sheriff's car that Owen had given him for his third birthday.

The sight almost broke Anna's heart.

She moved to the bed, carefully pried it from his

arms and set it next to him on the pillow. Pulling the blankets up around him, she tucked him in, kissed his cheek and thought about how blessed she was to have him.

He was her life. Her reason to be strong. When he smiled, she smiled. When he laughed, she laughed. And when he cried...

Helping him heal was more important than anything else right now.

She placed her palm against his narrow chest, feeling it rise and fall, hoping that his dreams were good ones. She was about to turn back to the door when she heard a car outside and went to the window, staring down at the street below.

As Frank had promised, a sheriff's patrol unit approached, slowing as it reached the house. The deputy shone a light across the yard before picking up speed and moving on.

But as it rolled away, Anna's gaze was drawn to a nearby street lamp and the pool of light beneath it.

There was a familiar-looking black motorcycle parked there. A Harley.

As the patrol car rounded the corner, the shadows behind the bike began to shift, and Anna once again felt her heart kick up as all the emotions she'd been battling tonight renewed their relentless attack on her.

Then Brody Carpenter stepped into the light and looked up toward the window.

Chapter Four

She was out the door and crossing toward him before she could even think. She'd forgotten her jacket, and the night air bit into her. She hugged herself to keep from shivering.

"What are you doing out here, Brody?"

He gestured to the porch behind her. "You left your door hanging open. Not a good idea."

"What do you want from me?"

"Same as that patrol unit," he said. "To make sure you're safe."

"Is that why you were at the mall tonight?"

He nodded. "More or less."

"So why *now?* You didn't seem to care much four years ago."

She could see that the words hit home, but she didn't regret them. Rational or not, the resentment she felt outweighed any gratitude she had for what he'd done tonight.

"I'm not here to ask for forgiveness," he said.

"And you're not about to get any." She moved in close. "You told the deputy you wanted to talk to me about Owen. Was that the truth?"

"Yes."

"Then tell me what's going on—or should I call Frank back and have him ask you?"

The lowest blow yet, but she didn't care. She *wanted* to hurt him.

"Look," he said, "can we go inside? It's getting colder and you'll freeze to death out here."

"I'm not sure I want you inside my house."

"Come on, Anna, this isn't about us. It's about Owen."

"How could you possibly know anything about him? You haven't seen him in years."

Brody looked at her. A look she remembered well from their days together. One that meant it was time to stop arguing and listen. This was serious business.

"Owen sent me a message just before he died. A message about you."

"Me?"

Brody nodded again. "That's why I came back, Anna. That's why I'm here."

HE SAT AT HER KITCHEN table, watching her put a kettle on the stove. She was still shivering. Her anger kept her from realizing just how cold she was.

It would take a while for the warmth of the kitchen

to settle into her bones, and he wanted more than anything to go to her right now and put his arms around her until the shivering stopped.

But he knew that would be a mistake.

Once she had the burner going, she turned to him. She was as breathtaking as ever.

"So what was Owen's message?"

"There wasn't a whole lot to it," he told her. "And it came to me secondhand. I was in a refugee camp in Chad when I got it."

She was surprised. "Chad? As in Central Africa?"

He nodded. "The message came through the Red Cross. I was in an area called Farchana. I have no idea how Owen did it, but I guess he must have worked up a network of contacts over the years and somehow managed to locate me."

"What on earth were you doing in Africa?"

"Trying to help," Brody said. "After I left Cedarwood, I just wanted to get as far away from my life as I possibly could. You know how bitter I was."

She didn't hide her own bitterness. "I guess I found out, didn't I?"

Brody released a breath, but it did little to assuage his guilt. "Look, Anna, I know how badly I hurt you, and I'll never forgive myself for it. Never. But I was in a different frame of mind back then. My entire world had been turned upside down and I just wanted to get away."

"Africa's away, all right."

"It didn't start there. That's just where I wound up."

"So where did you go?"

"My first stop was New York. I figured I could get lost in the crowd there, be as anonymous as possible. Nobody looking at me as if I were a disappointment."

Anna frowned. "Is that what you thought? That I considered you a disappointment?"

"No, not you. But a lot of people in Cedarwood did. People I once considered friends."

"You were *acquitted,* Brody. Everyone knew that."

The kettle started to boil. Anna turned off the burner then poured hot water into two cups and dunked a tea bag into each.

"Maybe so," Brody said, "but it sure didn't feel that way. My career was finished, I couldn't get work and I just didn't want to be a burden to anyone. Especially you. So I wound up in New York. And after a few months there, I ran into an old college friend who set me up overseas. In London."

Anna carried the cups to the table, a renewed look of surprise on her face. "London? What did you do there?"

"Bodyguard work, mostly."

"For who?"

"I had a lot of clients. Actors, businessmen, politicians. You ever heard of Clive Banks?"

She nodded. "The movie star."

"I worked for him on and off for a couple years. Premiere parties, public appearances, that kind of thing."

Anna sipped her tea. "I'd already given up on you by then. I was desperate to talk to you, and Owen had been trying to find you for months, but…"

She let the words trail and Brody once again felt guilt overcoming him. "I guess that's when Frank stepped in?"

"Can you blame him? He'd always had a thing for me. Ever since freshman year."

"Believe me, I know. And you?"

She hesitated. "Finish your story."

Brody finally took a sip of his own tea, its welcome warmth radiating through his body. "Between gigs with Banks, I started doing work for a British MP. One day I was sent to do the advance security for a humanitarian trip to a refugee camp in Chad, and when I got there, I was pretty devastated by what I saw."

The disenfranchised families, the hungry children. The desperation in their eyes.

"I guess I felt a kind of kinship with the people there. Their lives uprooted by genocide. My own problems were so pale in comparison, it wasn't even funny." He took another sip. "So I quit the security

gig right then and there. Joined in the effort to pull
refugees out of Darfur and smuggle them across the
border. And that's what I'd just finished doing when
Owen's message came."

"When was this?"

"Less than a week ago."

"He was already dead by then."

Brody nodded. "I didn't know that at the time,
but yeah, the message probably passed through several different hands before it got to me. A Red Cross
worker had tried to deliver it earlier, but I was in
Darfur. I took the first flight home, but by the time
I got here Owen was already gone."

"So what was the message? What did he say?"

"Why don't I show you?"

Reaching into his shirt pocket, Brody pulled out a
small slip of paper. He had folded and unfolded it so
many times in the past few days that it was threatening to fall apart.

"It's brief and to the point," he said, "but it's the
reason I'm here."

He handed it to Anna and she pulled it open, staring down at the words that had been written by a
stranger's hand, dictated over a static-filled phone
line from several thousand miles away.

Brody knew those words by heart:

Trouble. Too late for me.
Protect Anna.
    Owen

ANNA SUCKED IN A BREATH.

These words only confirmed what she had suspected all along: Owen *hadn't* committed suicide. He'd been in trouble and someone had murdered him and staged the whole thing to make it look as if he'd shot himself in his own bed.

She had been right to question the official findings, and this note was proof of that.

Her scalp prickled and something toxic blossomed in her stomach, spreading through her bloodstream, making her whole body go numb.

"My God," she said. "We have to show this to Frank."

Brody shook his head. "Consider the source. He's never thought much of me and he'll probably think I'm running some kind of scam."

"Well, I don't. And he'll listen to me."

"Oh? Has he so far?"

The question gave Anna pause.

"You knew Owen better than anyone," Brody said, "and I can't believe this is the first time you've considered he didn't take his own life. You must have mentioned it to Frank."

She nodded. "He thinks my doubts are all part of the grieving process, but this should convince him he's wrong."

"Come on, Anna, you know how he is. He'll take one look at that thing and either call foul or claim it's some kind of suicide note."

Anna looked at the worn sheet of paper again.

Trouble.

Too late for me.

If you read these words with the preconceived notion that Owen had killed himself, then yes, Brody was right. But there were other things to consider, as well.

"What about the men who attacked me?" she asked. "I told Frank I thought they had something to do with Owen."

"And I have no doubt that they did. But I'd lay odds that if you show Frank that note, it'll only convince him he's right." Brody paused. "Worse yet, he may try to stop us from finding out what really happened."

Anna's heart froze in her chest.

Had he really just said what she thought he had?

"What are you telling me?"

"I may be a little rusty, but I still know my way around an investigation, and I still know how to follow my instincts."

"Then you'll look into Owen's death?"

"My first priority is protecting you. Just like your brother asked me to. So you've got a bodyguard whether you want one or not."

"I don't care about me," she said. "What about Owen?"

Brody looked directly at her now, his expression dark, his gaze unwavering, and she knew he wasn't playing games, wasn't making idle conversation or halfhearted promises.

He was deadly serious. And anyone listening to him should pay very close attention.

"As far as I'm concerned," he said, "the best friend I ever had was brutally murdered in his own home. And I'm not about to let those punks get away with it."

Chapter Five

Anna had offered to put him up in Owen's room, but Brody wasn't about to let himself be confined.

He wasn't here for a sleepover.

His mission was to protect and defend, and if Anna's attackers were to track her here and show up in the middle of the night, he needed to be ready for them. He didn't expect another attempt so soon, but it didn't hurt to be prepared.

After telling Anna to get her mother safely into her own room, Brody took one of the kitchen chairs to the upstairs hallway and stationed himself near a window overlooking the street.

It was past two in the morning when they finally said good-night, and the sky seemed darker somehow, as if a storm might be coming. Cedarwood had thankfully been free of snow since Brody had arrived, but he had to wonder if it would soon be falling, or if the turbulence in the air was a signal of another kind of storm altogether.

Brody decided to allow himself to doze, but nothing more than that. Catnaps would keep him fresh and alert. The tea would help, too, but before they'd left the kitchen, Anna had surprised him by preparing a thermos full of coffee for him.

It was a ritual she had performed at least a hundred times in the past, back when they had lived together in their small apartment downtown. Brody would be heading out on night patrol and Anna would stand by the doorway, holding the thermos out to him.

"Come back to me in one piece," she'd say then pull him into an embrace, kissing him, pressing her body against his as if to remind him what he'd be coming home to.

Not that he'd ever needed a reminder.

This time, however, there was no embrace. No press of the body. She had filled the thermos and set it on the kitchen table without comment, not quite willing to look him in the eye—as if she, too, remembered those nights but wasn't sure she really wanted to.

Brody's regret was a festering wound in his gut. He knew it did him no good to obsess over the past, but if there was one thing he could change, one course of action he could go back to and revise…

Leaving her was his greatest mistake.

As he settled into the chair, the sheriff's patrol car did another drive-by. If it were up to him, the deputy would be sitting at the curb all night, but the department was undoubtedly stretched thin. This was the best they could do.

He watched the car pass then sat back, looking toward the long hallway in front of him—the bathroom at the far end, the carpeted stairs to the left, the closed bedroom doors on the right.

The Sanford family home hadn't changed much over the years. He'd been up here many times as a teenager. First with Owen, the two of them reading comic books and playing video games, talking about girls at school. Then later with Anna, sneaking into her room late at night. A time that played in an endless loop in his mind: the anxious moments, the quiet kisses, the feverish exploration of each other's body. The feeling that they could never get enough.

Could never *give* enough.

Brody looked at Anna's bedroom door and saw light seeping out from the crack beneath it.

Still awake.

He couldn't help wondering what she was thinking as she lay in bed. About Owen, no doubt. About the men who had attacked her.

About him?

No matter how he tried, he couldn't keep from imagining himself throwing that door open and crossing toward her, tearing at his clothes as he moved, then pulling her off the bed and into his arms.

Feeling her lips pressed against his.

Her warm flesh…

He knew it was a pipe dream. Nothing more. But something ached inside him, a deep carnal desire that was difficult to ignore. It took everything he had to stay seated in that chair.

He had returned to Cedarwood three days ago and had been watching Anna from a distance ever since. He had told himself that he was merely fulfilling Owen's last wish, had come here only as a favor to his fallen friend.

But he knew that he was really here for Anna.

While he was gone, he'd kept tabs on her. Knew that she had married Frank and they'd had a son. He'd be the first to admit that he'd envied his old rival, had been torn apart knowing that Frank was sharing Anna's bed and raising her child. When word of the divorce finally reached him, he'd been saddened for her but overjoyed for himself, even though he knew he'd never take advantage of the situation. Returning home was not an option at the time. He had no desire to exploit Anna's loss, and there was too much pain involved for everyone concerned. Too much history.

But Owen's note had changed everything. Had given him an excuse to come home again.

Trouble. Too late for me.

Protect Anna.

That was his mantra now. Protecting Anna.

And finding the men who sent her brother to an early grave.

HE STRETCHED AT REGULAR intervals, but after a while, he realized he couldn't sit any longer. Too much nervous energy. He could blame the coffee, but he didn't think that was it.

He went downstairs and checked windows and doors as he turned the events of the night over and over in his mind, thinking about what he'd seen and heard as he sat on his Harley in the shadows of the mall's underground parking lot—

—Anna walking to her car.

—Santa Claus grabbing her.

—Her startled yelp as he pushed her toward the van, his voice echoing—

"The button. Where's the button?"

Santa had seemed desperate for an answer, and Brody wanted one, too.

What exactly *was* this button?

The only thing that came to mind were the buttons on a shirt, or a campaign souvenir, or maybe the power switch on a piece of electronic equipment. Or if you really wanted to stretch it: the protective knob on the end of a fencing foil—how was that for an obscure bit of knowledge?

Yet none of these fit.

"I know he gave it to you. Where is it?"

The *he* being Owen, of course. A point that Brody and Anna had agreed on when they rehashed the event.

Who else could it be? And if these creeps had known Owen well enough to make such an accusation, then Brody could only conclude that his friend had somehow gotten himself involved in some very bad business.

Trouble.

Too late for me.

But *why* was it too late? What had Owen done? What did he know that had pitted him against these men?

Had he stolen from them? Was this button a rare artifact of some kind? An antique that was valuable enough to kill for? Enough to make grabbing Anna seem like a reasonable way to obtain it?

And if this were true, and if Owen had passed it on to her, then why didn't Anna know this? Why was she completely clueless about it?

Brody had met Owen when they were juniors in high school. Brody's family had recently moved from another district, and he and Owen had become fast friends when they both tried out for the varsity football team.

After practice most days, they would grab sodas from a nearby Frostee's then hike across the street

his face up, as if remembering something, then said, "You ride a motorcycle."

Brody was surprised. "That's right. How did you know?"

"Uncle Owen showed me your picture. He had it in his wallet."

Brody felt the stab of grief. He knew exactly the photograph Adam was talking about. It was a shot of him and Owen down in Nuevo Laredo, after a long weekend of barhopping to celebrate Owen's new job with Northboard Industries. Anna had been scheduled to join them, but she had caught a cold just before the trip and had insisted they go without her.

They had both been wiped out when the photo was taken, not looking forward to the twenty-hour ride back to Cedarwood. And it was shortly after their return that Brody's troubles with the department began.

"My daddy drives a sheriff's car," Adam said, as if somehow picking up on Brody's thoughts. "Uncle Owen says he's one of the best deputies ever."

Brody assumed that Owen was being charitable when he'd said that. Owen had never thought much of Frank, and Brody knew the marriage to Anna must have been a tough pill for his friend to swallow. Frank *was* a good deputy, but Brody couldn't imagine Owen ever admitting that out loud. Maybe it was easier to say it to a three-year-old child.

Whatever the case, this boy was about the cutest thing Brody had ever seen, and he felt an instant warmth toward the little guy.

Frank must be very proud, he thought.

Brody got to his feet. "So you've never had chocolate chip pancakes, huh?"

Adam shook his head.

"Well, you don't know what you've been missing, my friend. What d'you say we go down to the kitchen and see if we can whip us up a batch?"

"Really?"

"I'll even let you pour in the chips."

A slow smile crept into Adam's face, reaching all the way up to his eyes, and at that moment Brody knew that he had made a friend forever.

He stood up, patted the boy's head. "Let's get to it."

ANNA AWOKE THAT MORNING to the sound of Adam's laughter. His familiar high-pitched trill floated up from downstairs, muffled but clearly identifiable behind her bedroom door.

It was a sound she hadn't heard in over a week.

Climbing out of bed, she pulled her robe on then padded to her door and opened it. Brody's chair was empty, and she thought she heard *his* laugh, too, coming from the kitchen.

What was going on?

When Anna got downstairs, her mother, Sylvia,

was sitting on the sofa, already dressed for the day, a sour, intolerant look on her face.

"When did *he* come back?"

"Mom, please, don't start."

"I can't believe you let that man in this house. After everything he put you through, you take him back with open arms?"

"It's not like that," Anna assured her. "He's here because of Owen. He heard what happened and he wants to help."

"Help himself right into those pants of yours."

"Oh, for God's sakes, Mom, nothing happened. We're long past all that."

"Are you?" Her mother looked skeptical. "I know how you feel about him, young lady. You've been carrying a torch since you were a teenager. Even after he deserted you. Even during that preposterous charade you and Frank called a—"

"*Enough,* Mother." Anna felt her face growing hot. "I know you're hurting about Owen, but that doesn't give you the right to be so cruel."

Sylvia caught herself, looked stricken, as if she'd suddenly realized the venom in her words. She brought a hand to her mouth as tears filled her eyes. "Oh my God, Anna. I'm so sorry."

Anna calmed herself. "It's okay, Mom. We're all on edge. But let's try to pull it together for Adam, all right? He needs us."

They both listened for a moment to Adam's

giggles. Then Anna said, "It sounds like he's feeling better. Maybe we should take our cue from him."

Sylvia nodded and wiped her tears with her shirt sleeve. "It's just so hard, hon. I miss your brother so much."

"I know you do. So do I."

She squeezed her mother's shoulder, forced a smile and finally got one in return.

Her smile disappeared, however, when she went to the kitchen and saw what Brody and Adam were up to. Brody stood at the table, stirring batter in a mixing bowl as Adam poured in a bag of chocolate chips.

They were making pancakes.

Brody's famous chocolate chip pancakes.

As they worked, there was a natural camaraderie between them, both smiling broadly, obviously enjoying this time together. A few of the chips spilled onto the table and Brody snatched one up, popping it into Adam's mouth.

"Good for the soul," he said, and Adam giggled.

Despite what Anna had just told her mother, this scene was simply too much to bear, and tears flooded her own eyes. She was suddenly awash in memories—memories of the life she had once dreamed of but had never come to pass.

A life with Brody.

She started to turn away. He looked up and saw her crying, his face reflecting surprise and concern.

"Anna?"

Then she was out the door and crossing toward the stairs, not wanting him to see her like this. She knew she was being ridiculous, that reality rarely matched the hopes and desires people often wrap themselves in, but she couldn't help herself. With sudden, gut-wrenching clarity, she realized that she would *never* have that dream.

Brody caught up to her on the stairs, grabbing her sleeve. "Anna? What's wrong?"

"What *isn't* wrong?" she cried, yanking her arm free, unable to keep the sarcasm at bay. "I'm happy you went out into the world and found yourself, Brody. I'm happy you were able to help people who needed it. But what about me? *I* needed you, too, and you were nowhere to be found."

She continued up the stairs, but Brody reached out and grabbed her sleeve again, stopping her.

"Anna, listen to me, please."

She turned. "I don't want to have this conversation. Let go."

"Not until you listen," he said. "I need you to listen."

She gave in. Didn't move. Just stood there, sniffing back her tears. Waiting.

"I can talk from now until forever," Brody continued, "but nothing I say will ever make up for what I did to you. I know that." He tried to clear the hoarseness that had overtaken his voice. "You don't know how many times I wanted to pick up the phone and beg for your forgiveness. To tell you how sorry I was. But I knew that wouldn't erase what I'd done."

"You could have tried," she said.

"Maybe. But I was so full of poison after the trial. Had become something I didn't want to be, and the last thing I wanted was to drag you down with me." He shook his head. "I was too stupid to realize that you were exactly what I needed. And by the time I finally *did,* it was too late."

Anna was silent. She could plainly see the regret in his eyes, but that didn't ease her pain, and Brody seemed to sense this.

"Saying I'm sorry will never be enough," he told her. "I know that. And I don't ever expect you to forgive me, but I'm not here for forgiveness. I'm here because Owen wanted me to be, and I'm hoping we can both put the past behind us and do what needs to be done to find his killers."

Anna said nothing. She knew he was right.

She looked at her mother, who still sat on the sofa, a fresh set of tears glistening. Anna knew that while she might not approve of Brody, she wanted an answer to her son's death just as much as they did.

This was a time for strength, not weakness. There were things Anna and Brody needed to talk about, yes. Things that needed to be said and understood— but now wasn't the time for it. The past was a distraction, and they had to focus their energy in another direction.

So despite the conflict still raging inside her, Anna nodded. "For Owen, then. But where do we start?"

"Same place I'd start any investigation," he said. "At the crime scene."

Chapter Six

Anna hadn't been to Owen's condo since before he died. She still had to pack up his things and either donate or move them to storage and possibly put the place up for sale, but she just didn't have the will to deal with it yet.

Frank had given her the number of a crime scene cleaning service, but she'd put off calling them and was starting to regret it. She had no idea what she and Brody might be walking into.

The condo was located in the center of town, a tall, modern tower of cement and glass that was well beyond Anna's budget. Until recently, Owen had worked in research and development for Northboard Industries, a weapons manufacturer with several lucrative government contracts, so money hadn't been an issue for him, and his choice of dwelling reflected that.

They rode there on Brody's Harley, Anna wearing her old helmet and doing her best to keep her memories at bay. She hadn't been on the back of a motorcycle since he left, and she was surprised to discover that she felt right at home, riding with her body pressed against his, her arms wrapped around his waist, the winter wind chafing her skin. She felt the familiar ripple of abs beneath her palms and would be lying if she'd told anyone it wasn't affecting her.

There had always been an undeniable chemistry between her and Brody, both mental and physical. That didn't mean she was planning to act on it—far from it—but she was well aware of its existence, and the feel of his body didn't exactly repulse her.

She had brought Owen's keys with her, but it turned out they didn't need them. When they stepped off the elevator, they both instinctively froze.

Down the hall, the crime scene tape had been pulled aside and Owen's door was ajar. It was open no more than a crack but was clearly visible from where they stood.

Anna glanced at Brody. "A break-in?"

"That would be my guess," he whispered then held up a hand, warning her back as he drew his gun from his waistband. "Stay here."

She watched him step toward the doorway, his body tense but fluid, moving with the assurance of a man who had done this kind of thing many times before. As he reached the end of the hall, he brought the gun up then nudged the door open with his foot and disappeared inside.

Anna waited. Felt a vague sense of panic rising.

What if Santa Claus and his van-driving partner were in there?

Her stomach tightened as she started running different scenarios and their possible outcomes through her mind—most of them bad. She half expected to hear gunshots and wondered how she should react if she did.

Should she flee?

Try to find building security?

Or try to help Brody somehow?

Her fears were put to rest when he stepped into the hall again and gestured to her.

"It's clear," he said. "But somebody's definitely been here."

Releasing a breath, Anna entered behind him. Owen's condo had always been immaculate, with sleek, postmodern furniture arranged in a way that gave the place a sense of spaciousness despite its relatively small size. Her brother had been something of a clean freak, and the condo usually reflected that—but not so much now. Now it was a mess. Furniture overturned. Stuffing ripped out of the sofa and chairs. Framed artwork and photographs torn from the walls and scattered on the floor. Drawers yanked open and emptied.

Completely trashed.

"Okay," Anna said, "that's it. We need to call Frank. He needs to see this."

"Don't waste your time," Brody told her. "He'll

just blame it on vandals. And we need to take a look around."

"For what?"

"The same thing the people who trashed this apartment were looking for. The button. I'm guessing they did this before they came after you, which means they didn't find it."

"And you think *we* can? We don't even know what it is."

"But if we get lucky and we can figure it out, we might be able to trace it back to its origin. And the more we know, the more likely we are to find the people who did this."

"That's a lot of *ifs*," Anna said.

"There are always a lot of *ifs* in a murder investigation. Doesn't mean we can't try." He gestured to the room. "You stay in here and I'll take the bedroom. Work a grid, look through everything. If anything jumps out at you, let me know."

"Like what?"

"A receipt, a key to a safe-deposit box. Or anything that might lead us to the identity of Santa Claus. A name, a photograph, a note. Something tangible."

"What about fingerprints? Won't we contaminate the scene?"

"Trust me, the people who did this didn't leave any prints. And yours are probably all over the place anyway. It's not like you've never been here before."

Anna nodded. That made sense.

Brody crossed toward the bedroom and stopped in the doorway. "And do yourself a favor and don't come in here. You won't like what you see."

Anna considered the weight of these words, unwanted images flashing through her mind:

Owen's bed.

Blood on the pillow. The headboard. The wall.

She didn't think the truth could be any worse than what she imagined, but she had no desire to see it and she nodded again. "Don't worry, I'll stay out here."

IT TOOK THEM NEARLY an hour to do the job.

Brody knew that finding the button or anything useful was a crapshoot, but he worked methodically anyway, scouring the bedroom section by section, going through the clothes scattered on the floor, checking beneath the mattress and under the bed, running his hands along the surfaces of the furniture, looking for indentations or holes or possible hidden compartments.

It wasn't until he reached the other side of the room—where Owen kept a desk—that he found two things of interest.

If Owen had a computer, it was gone. The drawers had all been yanked out, books and papers and office supplies scattered everywhere. But as he worked the grid, Brody found a crumpled sheet of paper and carefully flattened it out.

A bank receipt dated two weeks before Owen's death.

A five-thousand-dollar withdrawal.

This didn't necessarily mean anything on its own, but a moment later, Brody found a rectangular pad with cardboard backing lying facedown on the carpet. He flipped it over to discover that it was a desk calendar, Owen's daily notations scribbled in the numbered squares.

On the very same day as the bank withdrawal, Owen had written a time and address in blue ink.

A meeting of some kind?

Brody's initial feeling was that the withdrawal was a coincidence and that Owen was merely going in to interview for a new job. But the address was located in an area Brody knew quite well from his days as a patrol deputy—and was notoriously dangerous.

So what had Owen been up to? Why had he gone there?

A possible payoff? A purchase of some kind?

Drugs?

No, drugs didn't make any sense. Owen had been something of a health nut since high school, had always eaten right and taken good care of himself. He barely drank alcohol and he'd never picked up a cigarette in his life, so the idea that he'd go to the South Side looking for narcotics, or even a bag of weed, just didn't compute.

So why *had* he gone there?

Getting to his feet, Brody crossed to the doorway and stepped into the living room. Anna was sitting on the floor, surrounded by a pile of photographs that had been dumped from a drawer. She had one of the photos in hand and a cell phone to her ear.

"A couple hours early should do it," she said into the phone. "Thanks again, Trudy."

As she hung up, Brody glanced at the photo in her hands. It was a shot of Owen, Adam and her mother, all wearing broad smiles. Adam couldn't have been more than a year old in the photograph, and the sight of him touched something in Brody's heart. He felt it the moment he saw the boy's smile. Remembered how oddly adultlike Adam had seemed when he'd encountered him in the upstairs hallway.

Pulling himself from the distraction, Brody looked at Anna, nodding to the phone.

"What was that about?"

"Work problems," she said. "Did you find anything?"

"Maybe. Can you think of anyone your brother might know on the South Side? Any reason he'd go there?"

Anna considered the question and shook her head. "No. Why?"

He already knew the answer, but he had to ask anyway. "What about drugs? Do you know if he started taking them?"

Anna frowned. "No, of course he didn't. Owen wouldn't go near that stuff."

"I didn't think so, but according to his calendar, he had a meeting with someone in a very bad neighborhood. The same day he withdrew five grand from his bank account."

"You think it's significant?"

"Anything that raises questions right now is significant. Whether it'll pan out is anyone's guess, but I think we need to go there."

"Now?"

Brody nodded.

"Then you might have to go alone. One of my employees called in sick and I have to cover for her at the mall."

"You can't get someone else to do it?"

Anna shook her head. "Mom's watching Adam, and my other girl, Trudy, can't get in until later this afternoon, so it's either go to work or stay closed, and I can't afford to do that. I'll be there most of the day."

"Well, I'm not about to leave you alone," Brody said. "Especially at the mall."

"You'll be bored to death."

Brody showed her a smile. "I can tell you've never worked as a bodyguard before."

Chapter Seven

There was nothing even remotely boring about body-guard work. Brody had gotten some training during his days as a sheriff's cadet, but he'd really honed his skills on the job over the past few years and knew that the nature of the profession didn't allow you to be bored.

It was all in the eyes. They were constantly moving, constantly evaluating, always aware, always seeing what others paid little attention to.

He looked for anomalies. Signs of agitation. Checking faces, hands, unusual bulges in clothing. People wearing sunglasses when the weather or lighting didn't warrant it. Hiding their eyes.

Hiding their fear.

Fear was always a factor in crime, and very few people knew how to disguise it. A bodyguard was trained to recognize that fear, to notice that faint trickle of sweat rolling down a forehead on a winter night. The stiffness of a walk that would normally be fluid. A subtle hesitation in both movement and attitude.

It was impossible to be bored when both your eyes and your mind were working overtime, taking in everything while focusing on a single objective:

Protecting your client.

Trying to practice your trade in a mall, however, wasn't easy. Especially a mall three days before Christmas, overrun by last-minute shoppers, most of them in a hurry and anxious and irritated.

Then there were the hundreds of bags and boxes and purses of all sizes. Hands reaching into them, pulling out wallets, keys, cell phones, shopping lists.

You could never let your guard down.

Brody sat on a bench outside Anna's Body Essentials, carefully assessing each new customer who entered, not allowing himself to assume that they were harmless or that they'd be foolish to try to grab Anna in her own store.

He'd seen a lot of foolishness in his time.

Another important discipline for a bodyguard was the ability to stay focused while still allowing for the inevitable: a wandering mind. You had to learn to give in to that parallel line of thought that kept you sane while never letting it distract you from the objective.

As Brody looked around him at all the Christmas decor—the winking lights, the giant tree in the middle of the mall, the red and green bows, the wreaths—he was struck by the stark contrast between Cedarwood Mall and the refugee camp in Chad.

Last Christmas Eve, he'd been stuck in a tent, sharing a can of peaches by candlelight with a Red Cross worker, an attractive French woman named Sophie.

Brody was human and had not been a monk after he left Cedarwood. He had shared a bed or two, moments of intimacy that had never really gone anywhere, with women he had cared for, but never fulfilled him the way Anna had.

After he learned of her marriage to Frank, he seemed to be on some kind of quest to find her in another woman. And when that woman was ultimately unable to *be* Anna, he pulled away. Always a gentle release, but not something he was proud of.

That Christmas Eve, however, was anything but gentle. As he and Sophie made love, he'd gotten lost in the fantasy and called her Anna, putting an abrupt end to the moment.

The night had quickly gone downhill from there.

After that, Brody gave up women entirely. A year-long drought that only fueled his desire every time he looked at Anna now. He knew it wasn't meant to be, but that didn't keep him from wanting her.

HE WAS ABOUT FOUR HOURS into his watch when he was approached by two mall security guards. Unlike last night's duo, they were both big and hard and wore their uniforms well. There was an air of ex-military about them. Not the kind of guys you'd want to get into a scuffle with.

"Brody Carpenter?" the bigger of the two asked.

"That's right," Brody said then gestured. "You're blocking my view."

The two guards exchanged a glance then stepped aside slightly so that Brody could see Anna from where he was sitting. She was at the cash register now, ringing up a sale for a teenage girl.

"We'd like you to come with us."

"Am I breaking some kind of law? Have I been sitting here too long?"

"Frankly, sir, you could sit here until closing and I wouldn't really care. I'm just following orders."

"Whose orders?"

Now the second one spoke up, and he didn't seem amused by all the questions. "Let's go."

"Let me guess. Deputy Frank Matson?"

"All I know is they had badges. Now are you going to cooperate or do we need to get rough?"

Brody knew these guys were just doing their job, but he wasn't about to leave Anna alone. "I'm sure you both heard what happened to Ms. Sanford last night. So if you think I'm going to walk away from her right now, I'm afraid you're mistaken."

"That's why they sent two of us," the bigger one said. "Stokes here is gonna take your post."

Brody looked at the second guard. "I assume you know what you're doing?"

Stokes seemed annoyed. "Don't you worry, she'll be safe with me."

That was the problem, wasn't it? Brody couldn't help but worry. But Stokes looked like a guy who could handle himself, so he reluctantly got to his feet.

"Do me a favor," he said, "and take a position inside the shop."

The bigger one gestured to Stokes, and Stokes moved across the aisle and stationed himself just inside the entrance.

Brody turned to the partner. "Lead the way."

THEY WENT DOWN SOME stairs and took a long hallway to what looked like an employee break room. There was a refrigerator in the corner, a snack machine next to it, a bulletin board full of government notices and work-related memos, and several table-and-chair sets scattered throughout.

Frank Matson and Joe Wilson stood near one of the tables, looking exactly like what they were: a couple of plainclothes detectives who had seen it all and done quite a bit of it themselves.

When Brody entered, Frank gestured to a chair.

Brody crossed toward them and sat. "What can I do for you, Frank?"

"That's a loaded question," Matson said. He sank

into his own chair and leaned forward. "There're a lot of things you can do for me. The real question is, will you do them?"

"I'm a reasonable man."

"That you are, Carpenter. For all your faults, that's one thing I can say about you. With a couple of notable exceptions, you've always kept a level head."

"So I repeat," Brody said. "What can I do for you?"

Frank took a moment, as if he were trying to find a way to phrase his next sentence, but Brody already knew what was coming before he spoke. "I'll keep it simple. I want you out of here. Go back to wherever it is you came from and stay there."

"Why?"

"Because I know what kind of effect you have on Anna. She's been through enough these past few days. She doesn't need you dredging up all your ancient history."

"This doesn't have anything to do with history, Frank. It's all about the here and now."

"Who do you think you're kidding?"

Brody reached into his shirt pocket and pulled out Owen's note. "Anna wanted me to show this to you, but I told her it was a waste of time. Let's see who was right."

Frank took the note and unfolded it, reading Owen's words.

Then he looked up. "What is this?"

"A message from Owen."

Frank read it again then shrugged and handed it to Wilson. "So it's proof he committed suicide."

"That's what I told Anna you'd say, but that's not the way I see it. I think the trouble Owen was in got him killed and the attack on Anna last night confirms it."

Now Joe Wilson moved forward, getting into Brody's face. "What kind of scam are you running, Carpenter?"

"I don't know what you're talking about."

"I think it's pretty convenient you were in that parking garage when Anna was attacked."

"I was just doing what Owen asked me to."

Wilson waved the note in Brody's face. "And we're supposed to believe this just because you scribbled a few words on a piece of paper?"

"Not my handwriting, Joe. So don't even start."

"You know what I think?" Wilson said. "Maybe you had something to do with that attack last night. Maybe you been pal'in around with the wrong element. Like the guy in the Santa suit."

Brody smiled at him. "You never were much of a critical thinker, were you, Joe?"

Suddenly Wilson kicked out, knocking the chair out from under Brody. Brody fell back, slamming against the linoleum, and Wilson stepped over him, grabbing him by the shirt. "Tell us who they are, Carpenter."

Brody didn't resist. He knew he was being baited and didn't want to give them any reason to arrest him and haul him in. He just lay there, not moving.

"Like I said—I don't know what you're talking about."

"You're dirty, and we all know it." Wilson tightened his grip. "You gonna tell me you aren't part of—"

"Enough," Frank said suddenly. "Get off him, Joe."

Wilson looked up at his partner in surprise. "Come on, Frank, you know he's—"

"I said get off him."

Wilson scowled then released the shirt. He reluctantly stepped away as Frank helped Brody to his feet.

"I didn't want that to happen," Frank said. "You okay?"

Brody knew that this was *exactly* what Frank had wanted to happen. There was nothing spontaneous about it. The two had rehearsed the moment before Brody had walked into the room.

Nothing like a little intimidation to get a suspect to cooperate.

Or to scare him away.

And Brody knew that's what he was. A suspect. Not because of any evidence against him, but simply because Frank still cared about Anna and couldn't bear the thought that Brody was back in her life.

But there was nothing Frank could do about that, was there? And he knew it.

"Joe's never been the model of restraint," Brody said, "but I'll forgive him his transgressions. Are you two done with me now? I need to get back to work."

Frank frowned. "Think about what I said, Brody."

"About leaving town? Sorry to disappoint you, but Anna needs me right now."

"She needed you before and that didn't stop you."

Brody shook his head, smiled. "Now why did I know you'd go there?"

"She's my wife, Carpenter."

"*Ex*-wife, Frank. She doesn't share your name anymore and you've had a couple of years to get used to that fact. Why prolong your misery?"

The two men locked gazes, Brody knowing that Frank's anger was brimming, his brain working overtime, looking for an excuse to either arrest him or force him to leave town. There was no way Frank could do that, however, without upsetting Anna. And that wasn't an option for him.

Brody didn't really blame the guy. The heart wants what it wants.

But he had a job to do. "Are we done?"

Frank finally backed down. "Go on," he said with a dismissive flick of the hand. "Get out of here."

Brody stared at him for a moment then turned and walked out the door.

Chapter Eight

"Where did you disappear to?"

Anna had seen the two security guards approach Brody and watched one of them escort him away. She tried asking the one left behind about it, but the guard simply said, "I've been told to keep an eye on you."

Now her shift was over and she and Brody rode the elevator to the parking garage.

"Your ex-husband's feeling insecure," he said. "He wants me to leave town."

"Frank was here? At the mall?"

Brody nodded. "He's afraid I'll steal you way from him."

"Is that supposed to be a joke?"

"He's still in love with you, Anna. He and Wilson tried to cover it all by accusing me of being behind the attack last night, but that's about what it boiled down to. He thinks I'm some kind of threat to your relationship."

"Relationship?" Anna felt her hackles rise. She

reached into her purse and pulled out her cell phone. "I can't believe this. If anything, Frank should be thanking you for—"

Brody put a hand over hers. "Don't. You'll only aggravate him, and we can't afford any interference right now."

She thought about this then nodded and put the phone away. "I take it you didn't tell him about the money Owen withdrew? Or the address on his calendar?"

Brody shook his head. "He's already made up his mind about your brother."

"So instead of trying to do what's right, he wastes time harassing you."

"That pretty much sums it up," Brody said.

He looked at her as if he wanted to say something more but couldn't quite bring himself to do it. Then he plunged forward anyway. "Not that it's any of my business, but why did you two break up?"

Anna's stomach tightened. Such conversations were always a source of anxiety for her. She felt guilty about her failed marriage, even though the problems underlying the divorce had been mutual.

Frank's continued affection for her was obvious. Whenever she was around him, she got the feeling that he was waiting for her to respond to his cues, to fall into his arms and beg him for another try. But she knew that would never happen.

There was a time when she had fooled herself

into believing that she loved him, too, but it had become clear after only a year of marriage that she was simply going through the motions. Neither of them could give what the other needed, and a lifetime of banal pleasantries and passionless sex was not the future Anna had envisioned for herself.

It wasn't fair to Frank. Or her. Or Adam.

"You're right," she said to Brody. "It isn't any of your business."

And in that moment, she realized the depth of her fury toward Brody. If he hadn't left her, she never would have taken up with Frank, and there wouldn't *be* a failed marriage to fret over.

But she couldn't let that fury consume her now. What was the point? He was trying to help her.

And that counted for something, didn't it?

THE AREA AROUND FIRST Avenue and Pike was not one of Cedarwood's finer neighborhoods. At the edge of the industrial center of the city, it boasted more liquor stores and tattoo parlors in six square blocks than most people saw in a lifetime, and the women prowling the streets in spandex and short shorts were not charity workers looking for a donation.

Anna had come down this way only once, on a dare back in high school, and had been scared half to death by the experience. It was the last time she let peer pressure get the better of her.

Brody took a turn on Worthington, past a small,

boarded-up chapel that looked as if it hadn't seen business in over a decade. At the far end of the street was a grouping of old factory buildings, perched on the edge of the industrial section but long ago abandoned by anything having to do with industry.

Most of them were boarded up like the chapel, but one looked as if it might have some life to it, and Anna wasn't surprised when Brody came to a stop out front.

"Definitely not a job interview," he said.

A feeling of trepidation overcame Anna. "I can't even imagine why Owen would come here."

"There's only one way to find out."

The entrance to the building was along the left side. The door had been secured by a chain and padlock, but the padlock hung open and they were inside in only a matter of seconds.

What they found were the remnants of an old garment factory. Battered industrial sewing machines were laid out in two rows, covered with a thick film of dust. Spools of faded fabric were stacked in a corner alongside a cluster of rusty file cabinets. The only light filtered in through broken windows that hung high along the walls.

"Are you sure you got the address right?" Anna asked.

"I'm sure," Brody said, then he gestured to a set of steps across the room that led up to an enclosed office with an open doorway. A broom was leaning against the wall at the bottom, and the steps looked as if they'd recently been swept, a minimal bit of housekeeping by squatters.

They moved past the rows of sewing machines, then Brody cupped a hand next to his mouth and called up the stairs. "Hello? Is anyone home?"

No answer.

"Wait here," he said to Anna then moved cautiously up toward the doorway, his palm resting against the butt of the pistol in his waistband.

A moment later, he was peering inside. "Hello?"

He stood there a moment, scanning the room, then he relaxed and gestured for Anna to join him. She moved up the steps, that feeling of trepidation still percolating in the pit of her stomach.

It threatened to boil over when she stepped into the doorway.

The room beyond had been ransacked, just like Owen's condo, which pretty much confirmed that they were on the right track.

There was a cluttered workbench along one side of the room holding a computer and a bunch of electronic gear that Anna couldn't identify if her life depended on it. The floor was littered with more equipment and overturned drawers—the plastic, rectangular kind that her father used to have in their garage, full of screws and washers and other workshop doodads.

The doodads here, however, all seemed to be electronic. Transistors, circuit boards, switch components and other parts that were beyond Anna's vocabulary or comprehension. The person who occupied this space was obviously an electronics geek.

Brody flipped a switch on the wall and fluorescent lights came to life overhead.

"Looks like he managed to tap into the city's electrical grid. There's probably a functioning warehouse nearby whose owners are wondering why their energy bill is so high."

"So what is this place for?" Anna asked.

"I'm not sure. But he's working off the radar, so it's probably not entirely legal."

Brody crossed to the computer on the workbench and studied it. One side of the case had been removed, exposing the various components inside. To Anna, it was nothing more than a jumble of multicolored wires and circuitry, but Brody seemed to know what he was looking at.

"Hard drive is missing," he said, then he looked around at the rest of the mess, and spotted something of interest.

He moved to one of the plastic drawers on the floor and picked it up. A piece of masking tape above the handle had the word TAGS written across it in black marker.

Getting down on his haunches, he looked around the floor, running his fingers through the debris, but he didn't seem to be finding what he was looking for.

Then his gaze abruptly shifted to a leg of the workbench. Crossing to it, he bent down, pinched something between his fingers and held it up for Anna to see.

"I think I may have figured out what we're looking for."

It was a tiny, flat disk, about the size and thickness of a dime.

"The button? Is that it?"

"Hard to say, but I'd like to get a closer look at this thing."

"I don't understand," Anna said. "What is it?"

"I could be mistaken, but have you ever heard of an RFID tag?"

"RFID?"

"Radio frequency identification."

Anna shook her head.

"What about Owen?" Brody asked. "He ever mention anything about security devices?"

"Not a word. Why?"

"If I've got this thing figured right, Owen paid a visit to this guy with five thousand dollars in cash in his pocket. And like you said, he wasn't buying drugs."

Brody showed her the disk again. "He was buying one of these. And the simple fact that the drawer marked 'tags' is the only one that's completely empty leads me to believe that whoever trashed this place thought the same thing. Only they missed one."

"I still don't understand," Anna said. "How could that thing be worth five thousand dollars?"

"It may be worth a lot more than that." Brody pocketed the disk before taking Anna by the elbow. "Right now I think we'd better head out. It's getting late and we've spent enough time in this godforsaken neighborhood. It's not safe here after dark."

Anna didn't argue.

Her uneasiness hadn't waned, and the sooner they got out of here, the better she'd feel.

Brody flicked off the fluorescents and they moved together down the steps, Anna noting that the light from the windows was nearly gone now, the sewing machines little more than dark silhouettes in the dim room below. Someone could be hiding down there and they'd never know it.

As they reached the bottom of the steps, Brody tensed and moved in front of her, bringing his gun out again. A precautionary measure, she was sure, but a welcome one.

They continued past the sewing machines, Brody carrying himself like a man who was ready for just about anything. They reached the exit door without incident, however. No bogeymen jumped out of the darkness.

Anna let out small sigh of relief as they stepped outside, feeling her uneasiness dissipate as they moved around the building to Brody's bike.

But just as they pulled their helmets on and were

about to climb aboard, she heard the roar of an engine as a pair of headlights came to life—

——and a familiar green van headed straight for them.

Chapter Nine

Brody was in motion before he even saw the gun.

He pushed Anna to the ground as the guy in the passenger seat stuck an arm out his window and the weapon flashed. A bullet rocketed past Brody's head, gouging the wall behind him.

Shielding Anna, he brought his own gun up, returning fire.

Once. Twice. Three times—in quick succession.

The first shot clipped a side mirror, the second one went wild and the third punched through the windshield, hitting the driver in the center of his chest.

He slammed back against his seat then slumped forward, his foot falling heavily onto the accelerator.

The passenger—whom Brody assumed was Santa Claus—grabbed hold of the wheel, sheer panic on his face. But it was too late. The van shot forward and swerved sharply, the momentum tipping it onto its side.

It crashed down and slid toward an adjacent factory building, the scrape of metal against blacktop assaulting their ears. It smashed into the side of the building, knocking a hole through it, the impact rupturing the van's gas tank. Suddenly flames erupted, filling the air with thick, oily smoke.

Trapped, the thug formerly known as Santa crawled across the dead driver and tried to climb out his window, but something was holding him back.

"Help me!" he squealed. "Help!"

Quickly checking to make sure Anna wasn't hit, Brody sprang toward the van, the flames growing higher with every step he took. He leaped onto the vehicle, scrambled to the thug and yanked his arms.

"I'm stuck," the man screamed. "Pull harder!"

Brody doubled his efforts. "What are you people after? Who sent you?"

But the thug kept screaming, too blinded by panic to respond.

"Who sent you?"

The thug begged Brody for help, and Brody tugged at him with all his might, but the guy wouldn't budge.

"Brody!" Anna called from somewhere behind him, and he turned, realizing the flames had grown perilously high.

Smoke filled his lungs and he coughed, expelling as much of it as he possibly could, but he didn't let go of the thug's arms, trying desperately to shake him loose.

Then he felt Anna's hands on his waist, her fingers slipping into the belt loops of his jeans, tugging him back toward the blacktop.

"It's too late!" she shouted. "You can't do anything!"

Brody knew she was right, but he tried again anyway. He yanked with everything he had but it wasn't enough. As the flames grew even higher, threatening to consume him, Brody released the thug's arms and stumbled back as Anna dragged him away from the burning vehicle.

They were several yards clear when he felt a rumble under his feet and the gas tank finally exploded, sending up a ball of fire and smoke, the impact knocking Brody and Anna to the ground, abruptly cutting off the thug's tortured squeal.

They lay there, Anna wrapping her arms around him protectively as they watched the blackened shell of the van shudder and burn.

"Oh, my God," Anna murmured. "Oh, my God."

Then Brody turned to her and said, "I think it's finally time to call Frank."

THEY TOOK THEM BACK to the sheriff's office and put them in separate interrogation rooms.

Brody had been expecting this. It was the way

investigations worked. You were guilty until proved innocent, no matter what the courts might say. He also knew that despite being known to the deputies, he and Anna would be regarded with suspicion until the details of the incident had been discussed, analyzed and regurgitated. Again and again.

Brody was paired off with Joe Wilson, who sat him in a chair in the tiny room then left him to stew there for close to an hour before questioning him.

It was a technique that was supposed to wear a suspect down, but Brody had used it so many times himself in the old days that its effect on him was zilch. He leaned back in the chair and thought about that squealing thug trapped in the van, wishing he could have pried the guy loose before it had exploded.

Brody had seen enough death and torture overseas to have developed a strong aversion to it, and despite what Santa had tried to do to Anna, the fool hadn't deserved the fate he'd suffered. It also would have been nice to question the guy and hopefully gain some insight into Owen's death.

Did this mean the search for the killers was done? Were these guys the brains behind the crime, or had they simply been following orders?

Brody was banking on the latter. The two hadn't struck him as mental giants.

Identifying their bodies, however, would take time, patience and a certain amount of forensics skill. And if there were no dental records on file, and the van turned out to be stolen—which seemed likely—the department might never know who the two men were.

Which meant the investigation into Owen's death literally hit a wall before it had really gotten started.

Brody was thinking about what his next move might be when the door to the interrogation room flew open and Joe Wilson stepped inside.

"You should have taken our advice and left town, Carpenter."

Brody stared at him. He was really sick of Wilson's condescending tone. "No offense, Joe, but it'll have to snow in Bermuda before I ever take advice from you."

"See what that attitude's gotten you? Now you're looking straight down the barrel of a double-homicide rap."

"It was self-defense and you know it."

"Yeah? Where's your proof?"

"Come on, Joe. Just ask your partner's ex-wife. She'll corroborate. It was the same vehicle used in the attack against her and the same two guys. They shot first, and I did my job."

Wilson snorted. "Your job? I don't know if you noticed, hotshot, but you're not a deputy anymore."

"Thanks for the reminder," Brody said. He knew it was another attempt to get him riled up, make him do something he'd regret, but he didn't take the bait.

"Besides," Wilson continued, "all I saw at the crime scene was a burnt-out shell and two crispy critters. Nothing there that necessarily connects them to the attack on Anna."

"You're kidding me, right?"

"Videotape from the garage is pretty fuzzy, Carpenter. We got nothing on the driver and the other one was hiding behind that Santa suit. So we could be talking about two completely different guys. And for all I know, you're the one who shot first."

Brody was silent for a moment as he tamped down the heat rising in his chest. Then, in measured tones, he said, "Is this really the game you want to play?"

"To be honest? No. But those two goons are the least of your worries."

"What do you mean?"

Wilson pulled a manila folder out from under his arm and dropped it on the table. "Take a look."

Brody slid it toward him and opened it. Inside were autopsy photos. Shots of a guy in his mid-forties who looked as if he'd spent way too much time in the bathtub. His skin was bone-white, almost blue, and flaking off his body.

"We pulled this guy out of the river yesterday," Wilson said. "Take a guess what he did for a living."

"No idea." Brody had never seen the guy before.

"He was an electronics whiz who lived and worked in that garment factory you broke into." He paused.

"But you already knew that, didn't you?" He showed Brody a broad, self-satisfied grin that did little to hide the sneer behind it. "And that makes body number three, my friend. Looks like you just hit the trifecta."

ANNA WASN'T SURPRISED when Frank walked into the interrogation room.

He'd let her stew in here for a while, and that alone irritated her. But either he was oblivious or just didn't care. He seemed to be struggling with his own irritation.

He pulled a chair out and sat. "What the heck were you thinking, Anna?"

"What do you mean?"

"Going to the South Side? Getting involved in a shootout, for God's sakes?"

Anna sighed. "It's not as if we planned it. Those guys came out of nowhere. Just like last night."

"And if you weren't out there running around with that fool Carpenter…"

"What's the matter, Frank? Are you upset because he's doing what *you* won't do?"

Frank said nothing for a moment, clearly trying to put his irritation in check. He studied her patiently. "Carpenter's a loose cannon, Anna. He's interfering with an ongoing investigation—and so are you."

"What investigation? All you ever seem to do is

ask questions and file reports. Brody showed you the note he got from Owen and—"

"Have you told him the truth?"

The question stopped her. "About what?"

"Have you told him why you were so anxious to get hold of him in the months after he left?"

All the fight went out of Anna. Those months had been foremost in her mind lately, but she'd obscured them with thoughts of Owen. And she supposed her anger had prevented her from telling Brody what she'd wanted so desperately to tell him almost four years ago.

"Not yet," she said. "I've been working up to it."

This was a lie. She'd known she'd have to spill all of her secrets eventually, but she hadn't even tried at this point. The emotional price was just too heavy for her right now.

"Don't," Frank said suddenly.

"What?"

"Don't tell him. He's the one who ran out on you, and there's no reason he has to know."

"Come on, Frank, that wouldn't be fair. Sooner or later I'll have to."

"Why? So he can run away again?"

The thought made her heart heavy. "You don't know that's what he'd do."

"Don't I? I'm a simple man, Anna. When I look at the world, I like to strip it down to its essence. I do the same thing when I look at people. People like

Brody. When it came down to it, he took the coward's way out and left town, and I'll be damned if I'll let him do that to you again."

Anna frowned at him. "He's not a coward, Frank. That much I know."

Frank was quiet then reached across the table and took her hands in his. The move was unexpected, but she didn't pull away.

"Maybe you're right," he said. "Maybe I'm just being selfish. I tend to get that way when I want something."

"And what would that be?"

"You, babe. It's always been you. You know that." He ran his thumb along her knuckles. "We never quite took the way I hoped we would, and I know I wasn't much of a father to Adam. But maybe we can try again."

"Frank, don't…"

"My apartment seems so empty without the two of you. I keep thinking that if you give me a chance, maybe we can get it right this time." He paused. "In fact, I know we can."

Anna gently pulled her hands away. She might not love Frank, but she did care for him, and she had no desire to hurt him any more than necessary.

"You had your chance to get it right last night," she said softly. "But you wouldn't even take half a minute to come in and say good-night to Adam. Why would anything be different now?"

His expression sagged. It obviously hadn't even oc-curred to him that he'd made a mistake last night.

She thought about Brody and Adam making choc-olate chip pancakes and could not even imagine such a scene with Frank in the lead. His interest in Adam had been perfunctory at best. A means to an end for him. A promise that had remained unfulfilled.

The problem hadn't been that he wasn't much of a father. It was that he hadn't even *tried* to be a father at all.

"I'm sorry, Frank. I know you mean well, but I just can't be what you want me to be. I've moved on, and so should you."

Frank did a slow burn. She could see that despite her attempt to be gentle, it hadn't worked.

His humiliation was clear.

She was about to say something, a conciliatory gesture to help ease his pain, when there was a sharp knock on the door and Joe Wilson stuck his head inside.

Frank didn't look pleased. "What do you want?"

"Carpenter's a wash. I can't get anything out of him. I say we just book the creep and throw him in a—"

"Cut him loose," Frank snapped.

"What?"

He looked at Anna, and she knew that he was doing this for her. He got to his feet. "We're cutting them both loose and calling it self-defense."

"But what about—?"

"We've got no evidence to connect either of them to the electronics guy, and unless and until we do, they walk. You got me?"

Wilson pulled back slightly, jarred by Frank's abruptness, but he didn't argue.

"Sure," he said. "Consider it done."

Frank turned to Anna. Softened.

"You be careful out there, babe. And tell that boyfriend of yours, if he gets you hurt, he'll have to answer to me."

Then he pulled the door open, pushed past Wilson and left the room.

Chapter Ten

It was long past dark by the time they got to Anna's house.

She had called ahead to her mother, and after a series of disapproving sighs, Mom finally agreed to have dinner waiting for them.

Sylvia Sanford and Brody once had a terrific relationship. She'd known how much both Owen and Anna had loved him, and the feeling had carried over to her. She'd welcomed Brody as a second son.

During high school, Brody's own parents—who both worked for an airline—had traveled a lot, often leaving the seventeen-year-old at home to fend for himself. Brody had no siblings to spend time with, so he'd been lonely inside that big house, and Sylvia often invited him over for dinner.

This was long after Dad died, and Anna remembered that once the plates were cleared, Mom would always bring out the cards and give the three of them a hopeful look, wanting to play a game of Hearts.

All Anna and Brody wanted to do was spend time

alone, but Brody always obliged Sylvia, sometimes even insisting on a second round when the first was done.

When they got older and Brody graduated from the Cedarwood Sheriff's Academy, Mom was in the very front row, smiling and clapping as he received his badge. And when Brody had asked for her daughter's hand in marriage, Sylvia cried.

"I wish Walt could be here," she'd said then pulled him into her arms and hugged him for a full minute.

Anna had watched them from the top of the stairs, unable to keep from crying herself.

During the "crazy days"—as Mom often called them—when Brody's life was ripped apart by finger-pointing and relentless hounding by Internal Affairs investigators, Mom had been one of his staunchest supporters.

So when Brody had disappeared in the wake of it all, after telling Anna that he "needed to get away for a while," it had been Mom who defended him. She'd told Anna and Owen that he would be back, to give him the space he needed to heal.

That space, however, had stretched much wider and longer than any of them had expected. After months of no contact, after the wedding date came and went and they finally realized that Brody wasn't coming back after all—not anytime soon at least—Mom finally broke down.

She felt betrayed, she'd told Anna.

Bewildered and betrayed.

Brody was, she'd said at the time, dead to her. And after this pronouncement they all began to wonder if perhaps he really *was* dead. Nobody knew where he'd gone. Owen had had no luck contacting him. And that dull ache they felt in his absence eventually grew more tolerable.

Adam's birth and Anna's marriage to Frank had helped, of course, but like Owen, Sylvia had never particularly liked Frank and his presence in their lives was no substitute for the real thing.

Bottom line, despite the betrayal, the broken trust, they all still loved Brody, and he was never very far from their hearts and minds.

They had learned, however, that the line that separated love and hate was a very thin one indeed.

ANNA KNEW THAT HER mother's fury was at least equal to her own. So getting her to agree to serve dinner to Brody tonight had been a minor miracle.

When they got home she remained stoic but civil, even sat down at the table with them. And to Anna's surprise, she had cooked Brody's favorite—meat loaf with mashed potatoes and gravy—which led Anna to wonder just how angry her mother really was.

Maybe the protests had all been for show. Now that the initial shock of his return had been absorbed, perhaps in the wake of their tragedy, Brody's staunchest supporter was willing to forgive—if not completely forget.

Anna's father, who was one of the most well-read men she'd ever known, had once said something to her that she'd always remember. She must have been ten years old at the time, and she had just caught her best friend stealing money out of the piggy bank in her room. The betrayal had been devastating, and she remembered crying in her father's arms, telling him how much she now hated the girl. Her father, who had been fond of quoting poets and writers and famous politicians, suggested Anna find a place in her heart to forgive her friend.

When Anna balked, her father shook his head and said, "Without forgiveness, sweetie, there's no future." Then he'd tucked her into bed, kissed her forehead and promised her that the sooner she learned to forgive, the faster she'd heal.

Many years later, Anna found those words—or words very similar—in a book of quotations boxed in the attic, attributed to the Reverend Desmond Tutu.

Without forgiveness there is no future.

Seeing them again only reinforced the sentiment behind them, and Anna now wondered if she should take heed.

Maybe the good reverend—and her father—were on to something.

THE CONVERSATION AT dinner was stiff but cordial. They stuck to small talk, mostly because they were all too raw to talk about anything else.

After a while they began to loosen up, lapsing into reminiscences about their younger years—before the "crazy days" came upon them—when Brody and Owen were playing football at Cedarwood High and Anna was on the cheerleading squad.

There was a kind of sweet melancholy to the moment, punctuated by knowing glances, and the elephant in the room was the empty chair across the table.

After a while, Mom finally gave in and nodded to that chair, a broken smile on her face.

Her voice wavered as she spoke. "He missed you so much, Brody. We all did."

Brody nodded absently then spent a long moment staring at the food on his plate.

When he finally looked up again, he said, "This may be a bit hard for you to swallow, but the Sanford family was the best thing that ever happened to me." He sighed. "I can't believe I threw it all away."

Without hesitating, Sylvia said, "Neither can we."

And suddenly they were all laughing, her words so unexpected yet so true, they found themselves doubled over. It was, Anna thought, a cleansing of the soul. A regeneration of the spirit. A brief but welcome return to what they'd once been.

As the moment subsided, a small voice said, "Why are you guys laughing?" and they turned to find Adam standing at the foot of the stairs, only half awake and rubbing his eyes.

Brody took one look at him, broke into a wide smile and patted his lap. "Come here, tiger."

To Anna's surprise, Adam didn't hesitate. He scooted across the room, climbed into Brody's lap and snuggled against him as if it were the most natural thing in the world.

Anna felt a hitch in her throat.

She glanced at her mother and Mom had that knowing look in her eye, the one that told her it was time for some housekeeping. The world wouldn't be right until Anna had swept all the corners and dusted all the windowsills.

But Anna wasn't sure she was up to it just yet. She had to wait for the right moment.

"I'm hungry," Adam said, his eyes on all the food.

Sylvia frowned at him. "You already had your dinner, young man. You're supposed to be asleep."

"How come you guys get to stay up?"

"That's a good question," Brody said, ruffling Adam's hair. "After the day we've had, we should all probably go straight to bed."

Adam looked up at him. "Are you gonna sleep in the chair again?"

Another good question, Anna thought. Now that Santa and his partner were dead, was it still necessary for Brody to keep vigil, or was the threat against her gone?

They didn't know exactly what the two thugs had wanted from her and why, or what Owen's involvement with them had been, and they certainly didn't know if there were other bad guys in the picture.

So was she safe now?

She definitely felt safer with Brody around, but until they had more answers, she doubted she'd be able to completely relax.

Before they left the sheriff's office, Frank had made noises about continuing to investigate. He'd even reluctantly agreed that the events of the day may cast new light on Owen's suicide, but Anna knew from hard experience that Frank's word could never be completely relied upon.

"I think," Sylvia said to her grandson, "that we can probably find a spare bed. Maybe Uncle Owen's old room." She turned to Brody. "Would that be all right with you?"

The offer was not an insignificant one. Mom had just extended the ultimate olive branch, and the look on Brody's face told Anna that he was both humbled and grateful.

"More than all right," he said softly. "I'd be honored."

UNLIKE MANY PARENTS after their children leave the nest, Sylvia had not turned her son's room into a study or TV room or sewing den. She'd kept it pretty much the same as Brody remembered it, complete with posters on the wall, gaming console, TV atop the battered oak desk and the stack of comics piled knee-high in one corner.

Brody went to the stack, pulled an X-Men off the top and leafed through it, once again remembering the day he'd first met Anna and how she had taken his breath away the moment he saw her.

As if by magic, she appeared in the doorway carrying fresh sheets and blankets. Laying them atop the desk chair, she crossed to the bed and began stripping away the linen.

Brody dropped the comic book back on the stack and moved to help her. "You get the rug bunny squared away?"

"He's all bundled up with his sheriff's car in his arms. I swear he's practically attached to that thing."

Brody smiled. "I've gotta give you credit, kiddo. You and Frank really did something special there."

Anna smiled wistfully. "Me and Frank."

She looked as if she wanted to say something more then stopped herself. Her eyes clouded for a few brief seconds, then she seemed to shake away whatever it was that was bothering her. Brody knew her and Frank's relationship was none of his business. He wasn't sure why he'd even asked her before. He didn't really *want* to know about it.

Bundling the soiled sheets, Anna dropped them to the floor then reached past Brody for the fresh ones.

Heat radiated off her skin, and the close proximity of her body was just too much to resist.

He impulsively caught her waist in his arms, turning her toward him, looking into the face he'd cherished since he was seventeen.

She was startled by the move, but she didn't seem to mind. They stood there, saying nothing, the air between them charged with electricity. Brody considered that he might be risking a slap to the face, but he didn't care. He pulled her close, pressed his lips to hers—and they didn't tighten, didn't resist.

She seemed to need this as much as he did.

The kiss felt so familiar, so right, that he realized it was as unique to her as a fingerprint of a wanted man. No woman he had kissed before or since felt the same. The softness of her lips, the scent of her breath, the feel of her tongue against his...

They were all distinctly Anna.

His Anna.

"Mommy?"

They abruptly broke away from each other. Adam stood in the doorway, once again rubbing his eyes. He didn't seem to have noticed what they were up to.

"I can't sleep," he said.

Embarrassed, Anna involuntarily fluffed her hair

and straightened her clothes then started toward her son. "I'll read you a story."

Brody caught her arm.

"No," he said. "Let me do it." He looked at Adam. "Would that be okay with you, champ?"

The boy's face lit up. "Yeah! Can we read X-Men?"

"I don't see why not."

Grabbing the comic book from atop the stack, he slipped past Anna—their gazes connecting—and followed Adam to his room.

Several minutes later, Anna appeared in Adam's doorway and said good-night. Brody saw the faraway look in her eyes and knew that the moment between them had passed. She'd had time to think about what just happened and decided it was a mistake.

At least that's what he thought he saw. He wasn't a mind reader.

Maybe she was just sad.

There was a lot of that going around these days.

Chapter Eleven

The men in the sedan had been watching the house for over two hours.

They'd seen lights go on and off, first downstairs, then upstairs, and they knew they were witnessing the routine of a household getting ready for bed.

"None of this makes any sense," the passenger said. "We should've done this days ago."

"We shouldn't be having to do this at all," the driver told him. "If Chercover and Sakey had done their jobs, we'd have that button by now."

"And what makes you think she's got it?"

"Because I saw it in the pipsqueak's eyes."

"Whose eyes? Sanford's?"

The driver nodded. "He wasn't cooperating. It didn't seem to even faze him that I was about to put a bullet in him, like he'd made his peace with God or something. But right before I pulled the trigger, I asked him if he'd given it to her and he kept shaking his head, telling me 'no, no'—but I could see in his eyes he was lying."

"And that's what you're going on? His *eyes?*"

"Trust me," the driver said. "She's got it and she knows it, and it's hidden somewhere in that house."

"It better be. It's almost Christmas Eve—and you know what that means."

"We'll make it. Don't you worry."

"Tell that to Chercover and Sakey."

"Chercover and Sakey were cowboys. Tearing up Sanford's apartment, tossing Caldwell in the river, making that ridiculous play in the parking lot. All that trouble and they wound up dead. I told them we needed to finesse this thing, but they wouldn't listen."

"Like you finessed it with Sanford?"

The driver said nothing. Just turned and looked at the other man.

The passenger held his hands up. "I'm just sayin'. If you'd let *me* have a crack at him, I would've gotten him to talk."

The driver shook his head. "Not without consequences. If he'd had any suspicious marks on his body, that would've opened up a whole new kettle of worms. And we can't afford that."

"Yeah? What do we do when they figure out who Chercover and Sakey really are?"

"It'll be long past party time by then," the driver said, "and we'll be very rich men."

"So you keep tellin' me."

"You don't believe me? I've already got a buyer

lined up ready to drop two mil on those schematics. If I can find another bidder, we can name our price."

"Not if we don't get that button." He gestured toward the house. "And I don't relish stumbling around in the dark, looking for a needle in a haystack. Especially when I'm not sure the needle's even *in* the haystack."

"Trust me, it's there."

"So's the scooter boy. How do you plan on dealing with *him?*"

"I don't. If we're careful, he won't even know we're there. None of them will."

"You sound pretty confident," the passenger said. "You sure these gizmos you got us will work?"

"They'll work. The tech demoed them for me. All we have to do is wait for the beep."

"Sounds like voodoo to me."

The driver shook his head again. "Simple electronics. We kill the lights, go in, snatch the prize and we're gone."

"And if scooter boy wakes up?"

The driver smiled. "We put him right back to sleep."

It was the thought of her kiss that kept him awake.

He could still taste her on his tongue. Feel her lips. The hunger in them.

Her scent lingered in the room, an intoxicating mix of cologne and sweat and pheromones.

He had tried closing his eyes, putting her from his mind, but after a full hour of sleeplessness, he finally gave up.

He kept seeing the look on her face as she stood in Adam's doorway. The sadness. The regret.

He knew she was conflicted. Knew that she wanted him, but she wasn't quite sure she was willing to go there again. To make that commitment.

Why should she? He hadn't proved to be all that reliable.

But he was older now, and he'd learned that there were a lot more important things in the world than his own battered ego. He'd spent the past few years kicking himself for his selfish, unthinking behavior toward Anna, and he knew full well that her last memory of him was of a man walking out the door, never to return.

How could he possibly erase that?

As much as Brody liked to tell himself that Anna was the same woman he remembered, the reality was that she had moved on. She had a different life now.

A business to run. A son to raise.

Frank's son.

The thought tore at him. If he had played things right, he would have been making chocolate chip cookies with his *own* boy. He and Anna would have created the family that he'd never really known. The family he'd never really *thought* about until he was welcomed into the Sanford home when he was barely a man himself.

It didn't really bother him that Adam was another man's son. Blood or no blood, he had taken to the boy right away. Felt an easy camaraderie with him. But while he sensed that Frank wasn't in the picture much, Brody had no doubt that if he were to stay in Anna's life, Frank would feel that old tug of rivalry, and things would get complicated very fast.

He wasn't sure he was willing to be the cause of that kind of friction. He'd already done enough to this family.

Yet as he lay there in Owen's bed, he couldn't stop thinking about that kiss. It had stirred something that had been dormant inside him for far too long.

He wanted Anna. Badly. So badly that he could hardly contain himself.

He didn't *want* to contain himself.

Impulsively, he got to his feet and went to the door. He didn't quite know what he was doing, what his plan was, his desire clouding all rational thought. Last night he had resisted the urge to go straight into Anna's room, but this was a different night now and he could no longer resist.

He opened Owen's door and stepped into the hallway. Anna's room was the last one on the right;

and he could see light coming from the crack at the bottom of her door.

Still awake.

He stopped thinking then. Didn't hesitate. Didn't evaluate. Didn't weigh his options and consider a course of action. Instead, he reacted. Simply aimed himself toward that light and moved. And when he reached the door, he grabbed the knob and pushed inside—

—and there was Anna, sitting on the edge of the bed as if she'd been waiting for him, wearing nothing but an unbuttoned shirt, one of his old uniform shirts from his early days on the force—the one she'd often be wearing when she handed him that thermos full of coffee at the door.

She looked like something from a fever dream, and Brody felt as if he had somehow stepped out of his own body and was observing this moment from another plane of existence.

Then her voice snapped him back to reality. She spoke softly, the underlying sadness still there.

"Why are you here, Brody? Why did you come back? What do you want from me?"

"I just want to make it right," he said.

"You can't. This will never work. I hate you too much. I'll never forgive you."

He nodded. "I know."

Then he went to her and pulled her into his arms.

A few moments later he was inside her—inside her body and her mind.

And he wanted to stay there.

Forever.

He just hoped she'd let him.

BRODY CAME AWAKE WHEN he heard the noise.

It was a subtle sound—nothing that would alarm the average Joe lying in an upstairs bedroom next to the woman he loved. Not a crash or the tinkling of broken glass or a stumbling thump or the creak of wood on the stairs.

But then Brody wasn't your average Joe. Just as he'd been trained to use his eyes, he had also learned to rely on his ears to alert him to signs of danger, and what he heard may have been subtle, but it was there.

A faint rustling. Nothing more.

Outside Anna's window.

It could have been the wind, but he knew it wasn't. A scurrying rodent, perhaps, but this particular rodent undoubtedly stood on two legs. There were bushes on this side of the house, and he knew that someone would have to squeeze past them to get to the electrical panel in the wall below the window.

A moment later the soft creak of a rusty hinge told him the panel door was being opened. There was a soft *thump,* then the digital clock on the side of the bed went blank.

Brody flew out of bed, grabbed his pants from the floor and yanked them on. Leaning toward Anna, he cupped his hand over her mouth and shook her awake.

She opened her eyes with a start, sucking in a quick breath. Brody put a finger to his lips, telling her to be quiet, then leaned in close and whispered in her ear.

"Get Adam and Sylvia and bring them in here. Move as quietly and as quickly as possible and hide in your closet."

He sensed that she wanted to say something, so he kept his hand cupped over her mouth.

"Someone's here," he told her. "You need to keep Adam safe."

She nodded, and he took his hand away. She got out of bed, her naked body silhouetted against the light from the window. Grabbing a robe from the closet, she pulled it on, wordlessly, then crossed to the door.

Brody snatched his gun off the nightstand and waited in the hallway as Anna moved silently to Sylvia's room then on to Adam's and brought them back. Adam was fast asleep on her shoulder, Sylvia blinking in fear and bewilderment as she followed her daughter into the bedroom.

After the three had squeezed into the closet and shut themselves inside, Brody closed the bedroom door then crept down the hall to the top of the stairs.

He waited.

Listened.

The house was silent.

Almost eerily so.

Then he heard it: the faint *snick* of a dead bolt lock.

The door at the side of the house.

Whoever this guy was, he was good. Not many people could pick a lock that fast.

And his presence here meant only one thing.

Just as Brody had suspected, the two guys in the van were not the last of it. And whomever they'd left behind still thought that Anna had the button. Or that it was somewhere inside this house.

And maybe that was true.

Or maybe it was right here in Brody's pocket. The RFID tag he'd found in the garment factory.

What the hell was on this thing?

He quietly flicked the safety off his gun and raised it, stepping sideways down the stairs. By the time he got to the bottom, he'd heard the door open and close—barely a whisper—followed by two pairs of shoes, thumping quietly on the polished wooden floor.

Not one man, but two.

If they split up, as he fully expected them to, Brody would be at a distinct disadvantage. His *only* advantage, he thought, was that they didn't yet know he was awake.

But even if he took one of them down, the other would still be roaming freely, and that just wouldn't stand.

He couldn't let either of them get up those stairs.

Not with Anna and her family up there.

Circling backwards he stepped into the shadows next to the stairway, where a tall Christmas tree stood, adorned with handmade ornaments, its lights dormant for the night.

He decided it was best to go on the defensive and wait these guys out. And just as he had expected, he heard their footfalls move in opposite directions, one heading toward the family room and kitchen, while the other came toward the carpeted steps.

A moment later, a dark silhouette emerged from a hallway and moved in his direction. Stepping deeper into the shadows, Brody waited as the man approached.

Only his eyes were visible through a ski mask, nothing more than two black dots in the wan moonlight filtering through the living room window.

The guy didn't seem to be in a hurry, one of his arms extended, holding a dark object in front of him.

Certainly not a flashlight.

A gun?

A knife?

It didn't look like either, but Brody couldn't be sure in this light. He'd have to be very careful when he took him down.

The man stopped for a moment, turning in his tracks, keeping the object extended in front of him. Then he continued toward the stairs.

When the man's foot hit the first step, Brody emerged from the shadows, circled around behind him and pressed the muzzle of his gun into the small of his back.

The guy froze.

"Two steps backwards," Brody whispered. "Very slowly."

The guy did as he was told. But as his foot came down to the floor, he shifted suddenly, feinting to Brody's left, then quickly moved to the right, bringing an elbow back, straight toward Brody's chest.

Anticipating the move, Brody stepped away and spun him around, grabbing hold of the wrist that held the weapon—or whatever it was—and driving the arm upward.

The man grunted and swung out again with his free arm, connecting with Brody's shoulder. Brody absorbed the impact and stumbled back, but it hadn't been enough to knock him down.

He started to bring his gun up again, but the guy charged, slamming him against the wall. The blow dazed him and the gun flew out of his hand and straight into a nearby table lamp. The lamp crashed to the floor, shattering against the wood.

A split second later, he heard running footsteps in the hall and knew the second guy was on his way and likely to be armed. Twisting away from his attacker, he swung out hard, slamming his forearm into the side of the man's head. The guy grunted and fell to one knee, but before Brody could move in for another blow—

—the second one emerged from the hallway—also wearing a ski mask—the black ugly silhouette of a gun in his hand.

As the gun came up, Brody dove.

The weapon flashed, once, twice, three times, narrowly missing Brody as he hit the floor and rolled behind the couch.

Three more shots were fired, punching the sofa cushions. Then, without a word spoken between them, the two thugs turned tail and ran, the hallway echoing the sound of their retreat.

Jumping to his feet, Brody found his own gun amidst the lamp debris, snatched it up and barreled toward the front door. Throwing it open, he ran out onto the lawn just in time to see the two men running down the street, jumping into a dark sedan.

As the engine roared to life, Brody sprinted toward the sidewalk, raising the gun.

But he didn't fire.

This was a family neighborhood, and despite the

hour, he had no intention of adding any of his own bullets to the chaos.

Instead, he watched the sedan burn a long patch of rubber as it tore down the street and disappeared. And he knew this wasn't the last he'd see of these guys.

Chapter Twelve

When the closet door opened, Anna nearly shot Brody's head off.

Once they'd closed themselves inside, she had handed Adam off to her mom and quickly searched the closet shelf for the shoe box containing her dad's old pistol and loaded magazine.

Anna fumbled in darkness, trying to snap the clip in place. Her father never had a chance to teach her how to shoot, but she knew he'd kept the gun for their protection. Years after he died she dug it out of the attic, but had never taken it out of the box until now.

The silence that followed the gunshots downstairs was excruciating. She had no idea what had happened and could only think the worst.

Had Brody been shot?

Was he dead?

The thought sent such a violent wave of horror through her that it took everything she had to keep from throwing the closet door open and crying out to him or running down to see if he was alive.

But she remained still, only the sound of her rapid breathing filling the silence.

Adam had miraculously slept through it all, but Mom looked as terrified as Anna felt. When they heard the door to the bedroom open and knew that someone was in the room, Anna tried to remain calm, but her knees began to buckle.

She brought the pistol up, her hands trembling uncontrollably, not knowing what to expect.

Could she pull the trigger if she had to?

Did she have that kind of courage?

If it meant protecting Adam, then yes, she would do what had to be done. But she didn't relish the thought of killing someone, no matter how heinous he might be.

A moment later, the closet door flew open and Anna came very close to squeezing off a shot. It took her a split second to realize that it was Brody standing there, but in that tiny moment of time, she almost put a bullet between his eyes.

He jumped back at the sight of the pistol. "Woah. Where'd you get that thing?"

Anna lowered it and fell into Brody's arms. "Oh my God, you're alive. Are you all right?"

He pulled her close, running his hands along her back. "My pride's a little bruised, but I'll survive. Unfortunately, the bad guys got away."

He stepped back now, letting them out of the closet, and gestured to the pistol. "You'd better put that where it belongs. There's been enough shooting around here for one night."

She nodded and immediately found the box and put the pistol away.

"Is it safe to take Adam to bed?" Sylvia asked.

Brody nodded. "They won't be coming back anytime soon."

As Mom carried Adam back to his room, Brody pulled out his cell phone and dialed. "This is Brody Carpenter. I need you to get Deputy Matson out of bed and over to his ex-wife's place right away. There's been an attack on her house." He looked at Anna. "There's no way Frank can ignore this thing now."

Anna only hoped he was right.

TWENTY MINUTES LATER, it seemed as if half the sheriff's deputies in Cedarwood County were inside Anna's house. Add the ballistics team to the mix, which was busy digging slugs out of the wall, and there was barely enough room to move.

It took Frank and Joe Wilson a while to show up. They both came in looking rumpled and only half awake, Frank studying the scene somberly—the broken lamp, the holes in the wall, the ruined sofa cushions. Then he approached Anna and Brody, who were sitting at the dining room table.

He gave Brody a look of mild disgust, then turned to Anna. "Can I speak to you in private, please?"

"You can talk in front of Brody," she said.

"I'd rather not. We need to interview you separately."

Anna glanced at Brody and he nodded, patting her hand. The gesture didn't get past Frank. He scowled at them then crossed into the kitchen, taking a seat at the table inside.

Anna didn't immediately follow. "Talk about déjà vu…"

"Go on," Brody told her. "It's standard procedure. Just answer his questions. We want him on our side."

Anna nodded, knowing Brody was right. But only a few hours ago she had been sitting in an interrogation room across from Frank and the situation hadn't been pleasant. She couldn't generate much excitement over the idea of a repeat performance. Especially so soon. Especially if it involved another "let's get back together" proposal.

Heaving a sigh, she got to her feet, crossed to the kitchen and stood in the doorway. "Well?"

"Have a seat," Frank said.

"I'd rather stand, thank you."

Frank waved dismissively. "Have it your way. But I just want you to know that the undersheriff has approved putting a couple of deputies at the doors.

Front and side." He paused. "And we're reopening Owen's case."

Anna was surprised. Brody had said this was bound to happen, considering tonight's turn of events, but she hadn't quite believed it.

"You're serious?"

"I don't joke about an investigation. You know that as well as anyone."

Anna sat at the table now, reaching across to take his hands in hers. "Thank you, Frank. Thank you."

He pulled his hands away. All business. "We still don't have IDs on the two guys in the van, but once we do, we're hoping we can find some kind of connection to Owen."

"Owen would never have anything to do with those creeps."

"Maybe it wasn't voluntary. Whatever the case, it looks like they wanted this button thing and their partners must be convinced Owen passed it on to you."

"I told you all this two nights ago."

"You still claiming you don't know what it is?"

Anna frowned at him. "Claiming?"

"Come on, Anna. You and Owen were like two peas in a pod. If he was in trouble, I can't imagine he wouldn't share something like that with you. Which is why you kept insisting it wasn't suicide."

Anna stiffened. "What are you saying, Frank? That I'm lying to you?"

"Maybe you just have some sort of misguided loyalty to Owen and think you need to cover for him. If he was involved in a crime—"

"Stop," Anna told him. "Don't even go there."

"It's just one theory of many, and I have to try them all. Are you sure Owen didn't give you something? Something to keep for him?"

"I already told you. No."

"A gift, maybe. Something you've forgotten about."

"How many times do I have to say this, Frank? He didn't give me anything. He didn't share any dark secrets, and I have no idea why he was killed. That's why I came to you. And that's why Brody's here."

The mention of Brody's name didn't make Frank happy. She could see that. While she was grateful that he was reopening Owen's case, she got the feeling that he was doing it grudgingly. That he wasn't completely convinced that Owen had been murdered. He was going through the motions because he'd been ordered to.

She had intended to tell him about the disk Brody found in the garment factory, but now she wondered if she should even bother. Frank would only insist that Brody give it to him, and she had a feeling that's the last they'd hear of it. That it would go into a plastic bag and be stuck in a box somewhere, never to be seen again.

Before dinner last night, Brody had called an

electronics guy he knew who had offered to see if he could help them figure out if the disk had any significance.

Would Frank do the same if it were in his possession?

Somehow she doubted it.

So basically what he was offering her was lip service and nothing more. Something he had always excelled at.

"Tell me what happened tonight," he said. "Start from the beginning."

She thought about it then told him, skipping over Brody's visit to her bed and picking up the story again at the point where Brody woke her up and told her to get Adam and her mother into the closet.

"Did he explain what was going on?"

"He just said someone was here. In the house."

"And how did he know this?"

"I don't know. He didn't say. I guess he heard a sound and reacted."

"Did you hear it, too?"

She shook her head. "I was fast asleep."

"So then you don't actually know if someone was in the house. You just took his word for it."

Anna looked at him, puzzled. She didn't like this line of questioning. "What are you getting at, Frank?"

He ignored her. "Where were you when the shots were fired?"

"Upstairs, in my closet, along with Mom and Adam."

"So nobody actually saw these so-called intruders fire at Brody."

"So-called?"

She just stared at him, not quite believing her ears. Was he serious about this? Did he think Brody had staged the whole thing?

Frank sighed and leaned back in his chair. "Look, Anna, I know you care about this guy, but I don't like what's shaping up here."

"Quit being cryptic, Frank. Get to the point."

"All right," he said. "When Joe and I had our little chat with Brody at the mall, Brody showed me a note he said he got from Owen."

"Right," Anna said. "So?"

"So if Owen managed somehow to locate Brody out in the middle of nowhere, who's to say they weren't in contact earlier?"

"Owen would have told me."

"Maybe, maybe not." Frank got to his feet and crossed to the stove. Grabbing the kettle, he went to the sink and filled it with water.

Although he was quite familiar with this kitchen, Anna thought he was being a bit presumptuous just helping himself like that.

He put the kettle on the burner and lit it. "What if I'm right? What if they were in contact earlier? What if Brody knows more than he's letting on? Maybe

Owen told him all about this button thing and he came here looking for it himself."

Anna was speechless. Even if she'd known how to react to this ridiculous notion, she wouldn't dignify it with a response.

Frank seemed to sense her frame of mind. He pulled the chair out again and sat.

"Just think about it," he said. "Brody shows up in town all of a sudden, just happens to be in the right place at the right time when you're attacked. So then he insinuates himself into your life, tries to get close to you again, because he's thinking the same thing those guys in the van were thinking. That you know where the button is."

"You're really stretching it, Frank. I know you don't like Brody, but do you even hear what you're saying?"

Frank shrugged. "He knows how to play you, babe. He always did. He gets you all gooey-eyed, you'll do just about anything for him."

Anna shook her head in disgust. "You're jealous. You always were."

He leaned toward her. "This doesn't have anything to do with me. I'm looking at this thing purely as a cop, and I don't like what I see. I thought the guy was clean back when the big storm came down, but maybe I was wrong. Maybe he was dirty then and he's dirty—"

Anna swung out, slapping Frank across the face.

Frank recoiled, bringing a hand to his cheek, anger filling his eyes.

"You just assaulted a sheriff's deputy," he said, barely able to control his fury.

No one else in the house seemed to notice what she'd done. Anna glanced at Brody, but he'd left the dining table and was talking to his deputy friend, Brett.

"I just slapped my idiot ex-husband who seems to think he's king of the world," she said. "And if you try even one more time to tell me that Brody had something to do with Owen's murder, it'll be a lot more than a slap."

"He's really got you snowed, doesn't he? What did he do? Tell you he loves you? That he's always loved you?" Frank shook his head. "He's just trying to get close to you again, so you'll give him what he wants."

"You have no idea what you're talking about."

Frank was about to bark a response when he paused, looking into Anna's eyes, seeing something there.

She had no idea what.

Then he said, "You slept with him, didn't you?"

Surprised by the question, Anna averted her gaze, felt her head prickle. She knew she was blushing. As wonderful as it was to be in Brody's arms again, she didn't quite know how she felt about it. Hadn't had time to evaluate and reflect.

The one thing she *did* know, however, was that Brody had nothing to do with these attacks, or with Owen's murder. That made about as much sense as the suicide.

"Well?" Frank asked. "You did, didn't you? You slept with him."

"That's none of your business," she said tersely then got to her feet. "You're way off base here, Frank, and I think you *know* that, but you're just trying to get a rise out of me. Your little bit of revenge for not wanting to get back with you."

"I just want to get to the truth."

"You want the truth?" Anna said. "I think it's *you* who's trying to take advantage of this situation. Which is nothing new. You came to me after Brody left, when I was vulnerable and needed someone, and you took advantage of *that* situation to fulfill some fantasy you'd had since high school."

"Now wait just a minute…"

"The truth is, Frank, you were a terrible husband, a terrible father to Adam, and as hard as I tried, I just never loved you." She could feel her legs trembling and her chest felt constricted. "If you think that's going to change now, you're crazy. So why don't you do us all a huge favor and just *leave me alone.*"

She left him there and headed for the doorway, hearing the sharp, high whistle of the tea kettle behind her.

Chapter Thirteen

The guy's name was Coffey.

Brody had met him in a criminology class at Cedarwood Community College, back when he was studying up for the detective's exam that would finally put him in the homicide division—the job Brody had been aiming for ever since he joined the department.

This was just a few months before Brody's entire career took a nosedive, and he hadn't really known Coffey all that well, but they'd bonded pretty fast and had even caught a few cold ones together after class.

When the accusations about bribes had started flying, Coffey had called Brody up and offered him his support. Said if Brody ever needed someone to vouch for him, he'd be all too happy to do it.

"You're a stand-up, guy," he'd said over the phone. "And the only way I can figure this is that somebody set you up. So watch your back, amigo."

Coffey wasn't a sheriff's deputy, but he was a true

genius when it came to anything involving transistors and wired or wireless components. He'd spent time working for the Cedarwood district attorney's office in their electronic surveillance department.

Brody didn't know what Coffey was up to these days, but when he'd tried the old cell number, his friend answered and seemed genuinely pleased to hear from him after all these years.

"Hey, hey, amigo. There's a voice I never thought I'd hear again."

"I don't think you're alone on that count. How you been, man?"

"Life is good, ever since I quit doing government work. I came into some money, so I opened up a chain of electronics stores that pretty much run themselves."

"Glad to hear it."

"Yeah, I can't complain. You in town long? Want to catch a beer or two?"

Brody cleared his throat. "Actually," he said, "I'm hoping you can help me with something. Your area of expertise."

"Oh? What's up?"

Brody told him about the RFID tag he'd found in the garment factory and asked if Coffey would be willing to take a look at it.

Coffey didn't hesitate. "For you? No problem."

"Thanks, man."

They made arrangements to meet the next afternoon at Coffey's place, and when Brody and Anna got there—feeling a little worn out after their ordeal with the thugs and the investigation that followed—they found a place that looked very much like a cleaner, neater version of the garment factory workshop.

A row of shelves and a long workbench dominated one side of the room, parts and equipment crowding most of the real estate. Coffey sat on a rollaway stool, hovering over a swing-arm magnifying lamp, staring intently at the minuscule speck of an electronic chip he'd caught between a pair of tweezers.

"I think it's blown," he said to Brody as they stepped inside the room. "Things are too darn fragile."

He stood up then and went to Brody, pulling him into a bear hug. "Good to see you, amigo. You're bigger than I remember. You been working out?"

Brody smiled. "I guess you could say that."

He introduced Anna and as they shook hands, Anna said, "I think we may've met briefly at a party a couple years ago. You were still working for the D.A., then."

Coffey studied her, then he grinned and nodded as the memory came back to him. "That's right. You're Frank Matson's wife."

"That was then, this is now," she said, and Coffey gave them a look that said he understood.

He gestured to Brody. "So where's this RFID tag you want to show me?"

Brody pulled the disk out of his pocket and handed it to him. Coffey held it up, giving it the once-over.

"Looks generic," he said. "Where'd you find it?"

"Place that looks a lot like this one, only in a much rougher neighborhood and with hacked electricity. I'm pretty sure he was working off the grid."

"You find any more?"

"No, but there was a drawer marked 'tags', and I have a feeling it once held a bunch of them."

Coffey nodded. "They're blanks. Ten to one this guy was making clones."

"Clones?" Anna asked. "Clones of what?"

"Radio-controlled security tags."

Anna frowned. "Brody mentioned that before. Security for what?"

Coffey went to his workbench and started rifling through the clutter.

"You ever have a job where the only way to get inside was through an electronically controlled door? There's no key, but there's a small box on the wall that you wave a card in front of?" He found what he was looking for and held it up. It was a blank credit card. No identifying marks. "One of these," he said.

Anna nodded. "I have one in my purse. I use it to get into the mall after hours."

Coffey held up the disk now. "This is essentially the same thing. A radio frequency identity tag—or button as it's called in the biz. They're usually inserted inside key chains, so that all you have to do is wave your keys in front of the lock to gain entry."

"It's not just limited to key chains," Brody said. "Wristwatches, cell phones, compacts, you name it."

"So I assume it has some kind of special code in it?" Anna asked.

"Right," Coffey said. "They're coded with a unique ID that not only corresponds with the lock but stores the identity of the user and records the date and time of his or her entry." He held up the disk again. "Now, since you say this came out of a drawer that was probably full of these things, I'm guessing it's blank. But since you say this guy in the lab was working off the grid, I've got a feeling he was making clones, which is a very lucrative business."

"So he was making clones of existing ID cards?"

Coffey nodded. "He'd have to spoof the ID itself, but it can be done. And if one of these things falls into the wrong hands, you've got the potential for some major larceny. Whatever lock it corresponds to has just been rendered useless."

Brody gestured to the disk. "Can you check that thing, see if there's anything on it?"

"I can try."

He moved to his bench, played around for a moment with some of the gear there then waved the button under it and shook his head. "Like I said—blank."

So it obviously wasn't the button they were looking for. Brody had hoped they'd get lucky, but he hadn't really been counting on it.

"If I wanted one of these clones made, how much would it cost me?"

Coffey frowned at him. "Sorry, amigo. You got the wrong guy. I'm not interested in going to prison."

"Relax, man, it's a hypothetical."

Coffey thought about it a moment, then said, "I guess if you want a sure thing—somebody who really knows what he's doing—you'd probably have to pay a few grand to get one."

Brody considered the withdrawal Owen had made shortly before visiting the garment factory. Five thousand dollars.

Had he been buying a clone?

And if so, why?

What lock was he trying to circumvent and how did Santa Claus and the other thugs figure into the equation?

Brody knew the clone must exist, otherwise people wouldn't be getting killed over it.

So where was it?

Somewhere in Anna's house?

In Owen's apartment?

Finding something so small in either place could be tough, if not impossible.

Unless you had assistance.

Brody thought back to the two thugs he'd tangled with that morning. Before he'd approached the one heading for the stairs, he'd noticed that the guy was carrying something that, at the time, he'd thought might be a weapon.

But what if it wasn't a weapon at all?

"If one of these tags was lost somewhere in my house," he said to Coffey, "is there a device I could use to home in on it? Make the search a little easier?"

"Sure," Coffey said. He crossed to a metal cabinet and opened the doors, revealing even more electronic gear stashed on its shelves. He rifled around for a moment and came back with a gray, rectangular device that was slightly larger than your average cell phone.

"This is a modified RFID reader," Coffey told them. "It's set to pick up any transmitter frequency within a three-foot range."

"How does it work?" Anna asked.

"You get close enough to your target and you'll know it." He flipped a switch on the side of the unit and extended his arm, moving toward the credit card tag on his workbench. As he got close, the device emitted a steady, high-pitched beep.

"Nice," Brody said. "You think we could borrow that?"

Coffey tossed the unit to Brody and it stopped

beeping. "Be my guest, amigo. Just make sure you turn it off when you're not using it. I don't know how long the battery will last." Then he grinned. "Oh, and don't get me in trouble."

Brody flicked the unit off and dropped it into his coat pocket.

"Wouldn't dream of it," he said.

Chapter Fourteen

When they got to Owen's place, they discovered that Frank hadn't been lying about reopening the case. The crime scene unit was parked out front, and several deputies were going in and out of the building.

"Bad timing," Brody told Anna. "They'll never let us into that apartment."

"So what do we do now?"

"Wait them out." He shifted his gaze to the sky. It was gray with clouds and threatening to burst. "It looks like a storm is coming, and I sure don't feel like waiting out here. I could use something hot to drink."

"We could go to the mall. Trudy's covering for me, but it wouldn't hurt to check in."

"Right before Christmas Eve? No thanks. I've had enough chaos for one day."

"Then where?"

Brody thought about it a moment. "How about Marlene's? Are they still in business?"

Anna's heart stuttered.

In the old days, Marlene's Diner had been one of their favorite haunts. They'd had their first date there, when, after months of endless flirting, Brody had finally mustered up the courage to ask her out.

The food at Marlene's was only passable and the Cokes were watered down, but none of this had registered that first awkward night, when all Anna could do was stare across the table at Brody while trying hard to pretend she wasn't madly in love with him. Admitting something like that was far too risky for a girl her age, especially when she wasn't sure how Brody had felt.

She knew by the end of the night.

As they lay in the darkness of her bedroom, in the afterglow of their first time together, Anna's heart pounding, her legs weak and trembling, her entire body still tingling with pleasure, she had known, with great certainty, that Brody was the boy—the man—she would be with forever.

Funny how things change.

MARLENE'S HADN'T CHANGED much, however. Anna hadn't been here in years, and it may have been a little worn around the edges, but it had the same red patent-leather booths, checkered tables and surly, disinterested waitresses.

They found their usual spot near the jukebox, both going to it automatically. Although the "forever" that Anna had dreamt of never materialized, the familiarity of the place took her back to those simpler days, when all she wanted was time alone with Brody.

After the waitress brought their coffee, he said, "I think we need to talk about what happened last night."

Anna was surprised. Brody had always been a doer, not a talker. A creature of impulse. And last night had certainly been an impulsive move for both of them—the product of nearly four years of pent-up desire that ended with the same pounding heart, the same weak and trembling legs, the same tingling of pleasure she got whenever she was with Brody.

But with everything that had happened since, she still hadn't had time to process the moment, and she wasn't sure she was ready to talk about it.

"Can't we just leave it alone?" she said. "Enjoy it for what it was?"

"What *was* it?"

Anna thought about this, shrugged. "Two old friends trying to comfort each other?"

Brody looked wounded. "Is that all it meant to you?"

"To be honest, Brody, I'm not sure. I'd be lying to you if I said I didn't want it. Or that I wish it hadn't happened. But we aren't kids anymore. We have different lives now." She sighed. "I still love you, you know. That'll probably never change. But I have complications in my life. There's Adam to think about and…"

She stopped herself.

Should she tell him the truth?

Could she?

"And what?" he asked.

Don't, Frank had said. *Don't tell him.*

Anna shook her head. She'd waited a long time for this moment, had tried desperately to contact Brody so that she could share the news, but now that the moment was finally here, now that they were sitting face-to-face, she couldn't bring herself to say it—just as she couldn't say it last night, when she lay in his arms.

This had nothing to do with what Frank had told her. Despite his overtures of late, she'd written him off long ago and his opinion had never been less important to her.

Still, she hesitated. Brody had a right to the truth—she knew that. But what she *didn't* know was where he'd be a week from now. Or a year.

Would he still be in Cedarwood?

Was this something she could count on?

The emotions swirling around them were too raw, too volatile to be introducing something new and unexpected into the mix, and her instincts told her that now just wasn't the time to broach the subject.

But if not now, when?

"Anna?"

"Nothing," she said. "It can wait."

Brody furrowed his brow at her. "What's going on? I keep feeling like you want to tell me something but you're holding back."

"It can wait," she said again then sipped her coffee in silence.

BY THE TIME THEY GOT back to Owen's apartment building, it was raining. Not hard, but Brody knew that they were only a thunderclap away from an all-out downpour.

The good news was that the deputies and CSI wagon were gone. Not really a surprise, he supposed, since there wasn't a whole lot of evidence to gather and the scene had been thoroughly contaminated, especially a week after the crime had taken place.

In fact, coming here again may well have been a waste of *their* time, but Brody believed in being thorough, and if that RFID tag was somewhere in Owen's condo, they had to find it.

He didn't expect the bodies in the van to be identified anytime soon, and that button—and the information encoded on it—was the only thing that might lead them to the truth.

After checking to make sure there weren't any stray deputies lingering, they made their way up to the fourteenth-floor hallway and saw a fresh new criss-cross of yellow crime scene tape blocking Owen's door.

Brody pulled it aside and turned to Anna. Ever since they'd left Marlene's she'd seemed subdued and preoccupied. He knew there were a number of things weighing on her mind right now, and he had decided to give her space.

He'd certainly taken enough of his own.

More than enough.

"Key?" he said.

She came out of her fog then dug around in her purse until she found one. Reaching past him, she unlocked the door and pushed it open.

Brody took the modified RFID reader from his pocket, switched it on then stepped into the living room, feeling Anna right behind him.

The place didn't look any different. Some of the clutter had been moved, and Brody was sure that the photographs Anna had found and any significant records or paperwork would have been bagged and tagged. But only a trained eye would know that anyone had been here since he and Anna had left the place yesterday.

He kept his arm extended and moved about the room, working his way past the sofa and chairs, the coffee table, the credenza against one wall, stepping gingerly around the contents of the drawers that had been dumped on the floor.

Nothing. The RFID reader remained silent.

They moved to the kitchen. The cabinets hung open and boxes of cereal, bags of flour and sugar

and canned goods were scattered across the linoleum, along with pots and pans and drawers full of
utensils.

Brody waved the device past all of them, crouching to get low to the floor.

Still nothing. The reader didn't beep.

They crossed to the bedroom. As it had yesterday, the door hung open, and Brody knew that Anna
wouldn't like what was waiting for them inside, so
he repeated his warning.

"You might want to hold back."

But she shook her head this time. "No. I want to
see. I want to know exactly what they did to him."

They stepped past the threshold, and as Anna
stood near the doorway, taking it all in with a look
of complete horror on her face, Brody moved about
the room, arm extended.

The sheets had been stripped off the bed, but there
was still a deep crimson stain on the mattress and
blood splatter on the headboard, painting a vivid
picture of the violence that had taken place in the
room.

There were a couple of trajectory markers, complete with string and flags, and Brody knew that the
crime scene techs were trying to establish whether
the gunshot wound had been self-inflicted.

In his opinion they should have done this the first
time around, and he blamed Frank for not following
through.

"You gonna be okay?" he asked Anna.

She had a dazed look in her eyes, but she nodded. "I think so."

He went back to his task, but still the RFID reader picked up nothing.

As he reached the clutter left by the ransacking of Owen's desk, he discovered something he'd missed before—probably because it hadn't held much significance at the time.

It was a pink, rectangular sheet of paper. The duplicate layer of a form that had apparently been filled out and submitted. The header at the top read NORTHBOARD INDUSTRIES, followed by a list of checkboxes, indicating the items that were returned upon Owen's separation from the company.

Anna had told Brody that Owen had been laid off shortly before his death, and his depression over the loss of his job had contributed to the idea that he had taken his own life.

All of the boxes had been checked off, and Owen's signature was scribbled across the line at the bottom, along with the date of submission. Nothing unusual here, but one of the listed items caught Brody's attention.

"Look at this," he said to Anna.

She tore her gaze away from the bed and crossed to him. He handed her the sheet of paper.

She took a quick glance. "What about it?"

"Item number three," he said.

She scanned the list slowly this time, her expression changing as it registered. "A key card."

Brody nodded. "Which would open just about any secure room in the Northboard building. I seem to remember that Owen had a pretty high clearance rating."

"He was one of their top engineers. But what are you trying to say?"

"Look at the date under his signature."

She did. "So?"

"He turned that key card in a few days after he withdrew the five grand and met with the guy at the garment factory. Ten to one the technology behind that card was RFID."

Anna's expression grew heated. This wasn't the reaction Brody had expected. "So you think that's what he was trying to have cloned? Is that what you're getting at?"

"It only makes sense."

"But why?"

"Come on, Anna, I think it's pretty obvious. Northboard is one of the premier weapons manufacturers in the United States, with more government contracts than either of us can count. There's a lot of information in that building, locked behind very secure doors, and access to that information would be worth a heckuva lot of money to interested parties."

"So let me understand this," Anna said, and he could see that the heat was rising. "You're telling me that Owen got his key card cloned because he planned on selling that access."

"I'm afraid that's what it looks like."

"You're saying my brother was a criminal."

"He'd just been laid off from his job," Brody said. "These are tough times, and he had a mortgage to pay, a pretty high one from the looks of this place. And even with his skills as an engineer, there was no guarantee he'd get a new job anytime soon."

Anna shook her head in disgust. "I can't believe I'm hearing this."

"What do you want me to do? Sugarcoat it?"

"I want you to listen to yourself. Owen was your best friend, for God's sakes. You know better than anyone that he wasn't some petty crook. He was a good man."

"Desperate times lead to desperate measures, Anna. And who knows, maybe he was coerced. The guys he was dealing with weren't playing patty-cake. Maybe after he got the card cloned, he had second thoughts. His conscience kicked in and he tried to back out on the deal, and he got himself killed because of it."

Anna's face was full of fury now. "I can't believe you're blaming him. You sound just like Frank."

"I'm a trained investigator. I have to call it like I see—"

"Owen stood *by you,* Brody. When people were saying the same kinds of things about you, he told them they were out of their minds. That you'd never take a bribe."

Brody sighed. "I know that, Anna. I couldn't have asked for a better friend. But we have to look at this thing logically. We can't discard the obvious because we cared about the guy."

"And why should I listen to you?"

"I'm just trying to get to the truth here."

"The truth?" Anna cried. "You want the truth? You're the guy who couldn't be honest enough to tell me you weren't coming back after you left. You're the guy who ran away when things got tough, because there weren't enough people like Owen around to support you." She tossed the pink slip at him now, her anger at its boiling point. "And you're the guy who abandoned his pregnant girlfriend when she needed him most."

There was a sudden stillness to the air as Brody just stared at her.

Pregnant?

Anna had been *pregnant?*

Then the realization came down on him like a crumbling brick wall. "Are you telling me that Adam…" He could barely get the words out. "…that Adam is mine?"

"I hate you," Anna said suddenly then turned and ran for the door.

Chapter Fifteen

By the time he got downstairs, the rain was coming down hard and Anna was already climbing into a cab.

Brody raced after it, calling out to her, but it was too late. The car pulled away from the curb, throwing up a wide splash of rainwater in its wake.

Brody crossed to his Harley, his mind full of regret and guilt—but most of all, joy.

Adam was his son.

Their son.

His and Anna's.

It killed Brody that he hadn't known that Anna was pregnant when he left. If he had, he'd never have dreamed of going anywhere.

He could only believe that she hadn't known, either. That the revelation had come in the month or so after he was gone, when he was impossible to get hold of. He could only imagine how she must have felt, holding this news and wanting so desperately to share it with him.

The thought made him heartsick. Ashamed. Angry at himself for being such a damned fool.

As he climbed aboard and kicked the bike's engine to life, he thought about the instant connection he'd had with Adam, that feeling of warmth and affection as they'd spoken in the upstairs hallway. That bonding of blood between man and boy.

He thought about chocolate chip pancakes and pulling the boy into his lap at the dinner table and reading X-Men to him later on that night. All that time he had believed Adam was another man's child—yet it didn't matter to him. The kinship between them was unmistakable. Maybe if he had taken a moment to do the math, he would have realized the obvious truth.

That Adam was his son.

His *son*.

The idea of this seemed so surreal to Brody that he couldn't quite wrap his head around it. As he pulled onto the road, he tried to picture the boy's face in his mind.

Did he see himself there?

Did Adam look like *him*?

He remembered finding Anna in those young eyes, and he realized that must have been part of what had drawn him to Adam in the first place. That, and the way the boy had carried himself with a kind of quiet confidence, the understated maturity that had always been part of Anna's DNA, and so lacking in his own.

All he wanted right now was to get to Anna's house, to see her and Adam, to do whatever it took to convince her to let him back into her life, to let him be a father to their son—even if she couldn't completely allow him into her own heart.

They could take it slow. Or fast. It didn't matter to Brody, as long as she gave him a second chance. Let him *prove* to her that he had grown, that his selfishness was a thing of the past and would never again keep them apart.

When it came down to it, Brody was tired of being alone. His long, self-imposed exile had made him realize that. And he could think of no better way to remedy the feeling than to get to know his blood. His boy.

His Adam.

HE WAS ABOUT TEN MILES AWAY from the house when he realized he was being followed.

The rain was coming down in sheets, and he had made the mistake of allowing himself to be distracted. Didn't notice the headlights behind him until it was almost too late.

He'd had to flip his visor up to keep the rain from obscuring his view, but he was riding against the wind and the drops came straight at his face, cold as ice, pummeling him without mercy.

The mirrors mounted on his handlebars were wet and blurred, but he could still see those headlights, turning when he turned, speeding up when he goosed the throttle and slowing down again when he eased off.

He couldn't see the driver's face or even make out the model of the car, but he had no doubt that it was following him.

And he wasn't entirely sure the driver cared if he knew this.

One of the thugs from last night.

Who else could it be?

Turning a corner, he found himself on a long, lonely straightaway bordered by a stone wall on one side and a grassy, overgrown field on the other. With the rain coming down so hard, however, the field looked more like swampland—something out of a gothic horror flick set in Florida or Louisiana.

He was traveling at a fairly decent clip, about half-way along the stretch of road—only a couple of miles now from Anna's house—

—when the car behind him made its move.

Without warning, the car swooped in directly behind him, getting a little too close for comfort.

Brody goosed the throttle and roared ahead, but the car rolled in close again, nearly kissing his rear tire.

Brody veered to the left and the headlights veered with him. He hammered the throttle now, shooting forward in a burst of speed, but the car didn't hesitate this time, keeping a steady, relentless pace behind him.

Brody knew they had to be doing at least ninety now, and the car wasn't breaking a sweat. Keeping up this kind of speed in the rain was a recipe for disaster, but he couldn't seem to shake this maniac off his tail.

He veered to the left and the car went with him. Then, as if it had just been dosed by a shot of adrenaline, it sprang forward with a roar and rammed into the back of his bike.

Bumper met tire, the hit rattling through Brody's bones. The Harley lurched and swerved, the force of the blow ripping him from the handlebars. He hurtled sideways, flipped once and landed in a puddle of mud at the side of the road, the back of his helmet slamming against the ground.

Somewhere at the periphery of his brain he heard his bike crashing as the car's brakes squeaked, bringing it to a skidding halt. Gears shifted and it went into reverse, pulling up alongside him.

A car door opened and closed, followed by footsteps, as a dark figure moved through the pouring rain toward Brody.

He squinted up at it—a man by the size of him— but his vision was blurred, and darkness was rapidly crowding in on him, threatening to take him away.

The man hovered over him a moment, as if he'd

felled an animal and was checking the extent of the damage. Then he turned and hustled back to his vehicle.

As the engine revved and the car tore down the street, Brody struggled to remain conscious. The rain cleared for a brief moment, allowing him a final, unfettered glimpse at the vehicle as darkness finally overcame him.

He was certain he'd seen that car before.

It belonged to Frank Matson.

Chapter Sixteen

He didn't know how much time had passed.

It could have been hours or minutes. There was no real way to tell. He never wore a watch, and when he reached into his pocket for his cell phone, he found that the impact had crushed it.

So all he knew was that he'd been out cold and now he was awake and his head felt as if it had been worked over by a jackhammer.

On steroids.

Considering the speed he'd been traveling, he figured it was a miracle he was alive. The mud and grass had softened the blow some, but moving didn't come without a cost.

Was anything broken?

He didn't think so.

But he knew that he was battered and bruised, and getting to his feet would not be an easy task. Shifting his weight to his left side, he put an arm out and pushed himself upright, staring out at the street.

There were no cars around. The stretch of road was

as vacant as a high school parking lot on a summer night, and he didn't expect anyone to be coming by anytime soon. Not in this weather.

The rain had subsided some but not quite enough, and from his vantage point here in the mud, he saw his overturned bike across the street, lying in the gutter, rainwater rushing past it. He couldn't tell the extent of the damage.

Had that really been Frank's car behind him?

He didn't know for sure.

The car had been similar, no doubt about it, but maybe he was projecting his own prejudice onto the situation. He'd never cared for the guy, but he'd never really thought of him as a violent man.

What reason would Frank have to try to kill him?

Because of Anna?

Out of jealousy?

That didn't seem likely. Yet here he lay, and the only decent glimpse of the car he'd managed to get had conjured up visions of Frank Matson behind the wheel. That didn't make it true, but he couldn't shake the feeling and something told him he could well be right.

Shifting his weight again, he rested both hands against the ground and climbed to his feet, wobbling slightly as his head began to spin.

The helmet had surely prevented his brain from winding up like his cell phone, but the pounding in his skull and the hollow light-headedness told him that some damage had been done.

He stood there a moment, the world swirling around him, and tried to maintain his balance.

His bike was only a few yards away, yet traveling that distance seemed like an insurmountable task. Pulling the thing upright and driving it away—even if he was lucky enough to find it still functioning—was not something he relished.

But what choice did he have?

Something in his gut told him that he needed to get moving. Whoever had mowed him down had obviously been following Anna and him, which meant she could be in danger.

Grave danger.

He needed to get to her house.

Praying for the world to stop spinning, he took a tentative step forward, his shoe sucking mud as he moved. He felt weak and helpless, like an invalid who had just fallen out of bed and was trying to figure a way to crawl back in.

Get a grip, Brody. You've been hurt before, so just shake it off and move.

Right, he thought.

Easier said than done.

Headlights appeared at the far end of the street, coming from the direction his attacker had gone. As they approached, Brody wondered for a moment if it was the same guy, checking to make sure the job was done. But as they drew closer, he realized it was a pickup truck.

The truck slowed and the driver rolled his window down. He was an elderly man with a deeply lined face and a kind of cornfield vibe to him.

"You okay, fella?"

It took Brody a moment to form a sentence. "Yeah…I think so."

The driver glanced across at Brody's bike. "Looks like you took a pretty bad spill there."

Brody nodded, and the effort made his brain slosh loosely inside his skull, sending a wave of nausea through him.

"The rain…" he managed. "I lost control."

The driver set his brake and put the truck in Park, then he climbed out and crossed to where Brody was standing. "I think I need to get you to a hospital."

"No," Brody said. "Just help me with my bike. I have to get home."

The driver glanced at the Harley again. "That thing ain't goin' nowhere anytime soon. And neither are you, from the looks of you."

"I'll be fine," Brody insisted, and he was already starting to feel a little better. His head wasn't pounding so hard, and the nausea had passed.

Now if only he could get the world to stop spinning.

"You're one of them stubborn fellas, aren't you? I've had a coupla farmhands like you. Think you're big and invulnerable, and you're too darn stupid to know when to lie down."

"No choice," Brody said.

"Man's always got a choice. But you're free to make the wrong one, whether I like it or not. Tell me where you wanna go and I'll take you there."

"I don't want to trouble you."

"Don't you worry about that," the driver told him. "I could use a little trouble in my life." He gestured to the truck. "Come on, let's get you in."

Putting an arm around Brody, the driver escorted him to the passenger side, pulled open the door and helped him into the cab.

Sitting down was the remedy Brody needed and he started to feel even better now, the world around him finally leveling off.

He felt his strength returning. A slow but steady recharging of the batteries.

The driver climbed in next to him and released the brake. "You sure you won't change your mind? Cedarwood General's only a few miles from here."

"I'm invulnerable, remember? Don't worry, I'll be fine."

The driver grinned. "Okay, Superman, where we headed?"

THE DRIVER DROPPED BRODY off a little more than a block from Anna's house. If his instincts were right and Anna was in danger, there was no point in announcing his arrival.

His only source of comfort was that Frank had posted a couple of deputies to watch over the place. But if his concerns about the man turned out to be true—if the car that had knocked him off the road had indeed been Frank's—then there was no telling what he might find when he got there.

The short drive seemed to have done him wonders. He felt almost whole again, his brain no longer banging around inside his skull. His body still ached, but he knew he could easily push past that pain, as long as he was fully cognizant.

"What time is it?" he asked the driver.

The old guy glanced at his watch. "Closing in on 7:00 p.m."

Brody nodded. He had lost more than an hour out there and was amazed that no one had come along before the driver had to scrape him up off the side of the road.

"Thanks for this," he said quietly.

"I'm a darn fool for doing it, I'll tell you that. I still think you belong in a hospital."

Brody popped his door open. "I hate hospitals."

"I guess you do," the driver said, then tipped an imaginary hat. "You stay dry out there."

Brody nodded again and climbed out, happy to find that he was able to stand now without wobbling. He closed his door then patted the side of the truck and watched it pull away, mentally sending up thanks for the kindness of strangers.

Pulling his collar up to help protect him from the rain, he pointed himself toward Anna's house and headed up the block.

When he got there, he knew his instincts hadn't been wrong.

There was a dead deputy on her doorstep.

Chapter Seventeen

The guy had a hole in his chest about the size of a cannonball, and his eyes were glassy and lifeless.

Brody tried for a pulse anyway.

Nothing.

He knew he should call this in, but not before checking the rest of the house. This guy needed a meat wagon, not an ambulance.

The front door was ajar. Brody reached to his waistband for his gun and discovered that he had lost it in the attack. It was probably lying in the mud somewhere along the roadside.

Glancing at the body, he noted that the deputy's gun was also gone, so he'd be doing this the hard way.

He stood very still, listening to the rain fall on the roof, trying to read the house, to get a sense of what he might be facing when he stepped inside. He inched up to the door and flattened against it, peeking in through the opening.

Nothing but darkness in there.

Except for the rain, the night was still and silent.

If he had to guess, he'd say that no one was home, and the thought of this both comforted and terrified him. It meant that there weren't any bad guys inside, but it also meant that Anna, Sylvia and Adam were gone, too.

And how they may have *gotten* gone was the terrifying part.

He could only hope that they'd somehow managed to run away or were hiding in an upstairs closet again, Anna nervously clutching the gun she'd pulled out of the shoe box, ready to blow the head off anyone who opened that closet door.

Not wanting to waste any more time, Brody brought a foot back, nudged the front door open then slipped inside and flattened against the wall in the foyer.

He felt vulnerable without a weapon, but what choice did he have?

He scanned the darkness. Saw no sign of movement. He had no idea how long ago the deputy was shot, but the body had still been warm to the touch—even with the chill in the air—so he knew it couldn't have been long.

Which gave him hope.

Not much, but it was something.

The only way to do this, he thought, was one room at a time.

Pushing away from the wall, he stepped cautiously

into the living room and looked off toward the kitchen. Keeping to the shadows, he crossed through the dining room and stopped just short of the kitchen doorway.

He stood still again.

Listening.

Waiting.

He heard only the faint ticking of a clock mounted on the wall above the kitchen table. He chanced a peek inside and saw that this room was also empty, everything in place, no evidence of a disturbance.

Except for one thing:

There was a half-eaten sandwich on a plate on the table, with a glass beside it, three-quarters full of milk.

A meal interrupted, Brody thought.

Adam's meal.

Not a good sign.

Stepping past the doorway, he quickly worked his way down the hall, hugging the wall as he went. After checking the family room and the downstairs bathroom, he moved on to a windowed door that led to a patio at the side of the house.

It was dark out there, but there was enough light from a nearby street lamp that he could see the body of the second deputy lying in a pool of blood.

His stomach roiled.

This was yet another bad sign.

He had hoped the second deputy had heard the

gunshot out front and managed to spirit the Sanfords away before the bad guys could get to them.

But that had only been wishful thinking.

His guess was that the deputies had been attacked simultaneously—probably by the same two men who had been here last night—and the chances that Anna and her family had gotten away were, at best, slim.

A wave of dread rolled through Brody as he left the door, moved back down the hall and circled around to the living room again.

He'd been inside the house a total of about two minutes, yet he felt as if he'd already lost too much time.

Moving past the Christmas tree, he started up the stairway to the second floor, hoping the Sanfords were hiding up there somewhere.

Please be in that closet, he thought.

Please just be there.

But as he reached the top of the stairs, the air up here was as quiet and undisturbed as the rest of the house, and the hope died inside him.

They weren't here.

He knew this. *Sensed* it.

But he had to try anyway.

He picked up speed now, crashing through the hallway from room to room, first Anna's—where the closet was dark and empty—then Sylvia's, and Owen's, and finally Adam's room—

—none of which showed any signs of life.

He looked across at Adam's bed, at the spot where he had sat the night before, reading the boy to sleep. The thought that Adam might be in harm's way was like a kick to the gut. But it was what was on that bed—what had been left behind—that really tore Brody apart.

The toy sheriff's car.

Sitting on the pillow.

He remembered Adam standing in the hallway, the car tucked under one arm.

My daddy drives a sheriff's car, he'd told Brody. *Uncle Owen says he's one of the best deputies ever.*

At the time, Brody had assumed that Uncle Owen had been talking about Frank Matson. But he realized now, with sudden clarity, that Owen had actually been talking about *him.* Had been trying to tell a son about his father.

A father who was missing in action.

Tears stung Brody's eyes, but he fought them back. This was no time for sentimentality or recriminations. The people he loved were out there somewhere, and he had to figure out how to get them back.

Still, that sheriff's car seemed to call to him. He felt the need to touch something that Adam had touched—something that meant so much to the boy—because he was suddenly afraid he might not get the chance to hold him again.

To know him.

He wanted to push that fear off as irrational, but he knew that the men they were dealing with were not shrinking violets, and they'd do what had to be done to get their hands on the thing they sought.

He couldn't let that happen.

Wouldn't let it.

Stepping forward, he moved to the bed and reached for the car, knowing that when he found the boy, Adam would want it with him. But as he got close, he was surprised by a sudden sound:

A steady *beep, beep, beep* filled the room.

Brody froze then jerked his gaze to his jacket pocket.

Shoving a hand inside, he pulled out the modified RFID reader that Coffey had given him and discovered that he'd forgotten to turn it off. It was a small miracle that the battery hadn't gone dead.

Holding it out in front of him, he waved it over the sheriff's car and the beeping sound grew in intensity, like a Geiger counter discovering a radioactive mine.

Turning it off, he tossed it aside and grabbed hold of the toy, then he moved to Adam's bed lamp and flicked it on.

Putting the car under the light, he carefully inspected it, looking for evidence of tampering—a gap in the metal or a loose screw. It was a clever hiding place. One that no one would ever think to check.

Staring at the wheels, he noticed that they were

about the same diameter as the security tag he'd found in the garment factory. Pulling each one from its axle, he pried them open, one by one.

He found what he was looking for on his third try: another RFID button.

The button.

This one worth the kind of money that men were willing to kill for.

Dropping it into his pocket, he haphazardly replaced the wheels and returned the car to the pillow. He had to strategize now. Figure a way to let the bad guys know what he had in his possession and bargain for the Sanfords' release.

Assuming, of course, they were still alive.

Please let them be alive.

Flicking off the bed lamp, he moved toward the door, but the moment he stepped past the threshold, the cold muzzle of a gun touched his temple.

"I want you to stand very still," Frank Matson said. "Or you won't be standing at all."

Chapter Eighteen

Frank pushed him face-first against the wall and patted him down. "You just bit off a whole chunka hurt, Carpenter."

"Cut the cop routine, Frank, I'm not buying it."

"What you've bought is a nice long stay at the state penitentiary. I've got two dead deputies downstairs, and it looks to me like I just caught me a killer. Where's Anna?"

"Why don't *you* tell me?"

Frank spun him around and pushed the gun in his face. "What's that supposed to mean?"

"Don't even bother, Matson. I know you're the one."

"The one what?"

"You made a mistake not making sure I was dead. I saw your car. I saw you drive away."

Frank scowled at him. "What're you, high on something? I don't know what you're talking about."

"Go ahead. Play dumb. But if you hurt Anna or Adam, I'll kill you. Plain and simple."

Frank stared at him then lowered the gun, a puzzled look on his face. "Maybe you'd better back up a little. What are you trying to tell me?"

"I'm not an idiot. I know you're behind all this—Owen, the attacks on Anna, the break-in last night. All because you want to get your hands on Owen's little souvenir."

Frank snorted. "And here I was thinking the same thing about you."

"I know Owen didn't like you much," Brody said. "So how'd you talk him into cloning his security card? You threaten him? Tell him you'd hurt Anna and Adam? Northboard must be holding some pretty valuable property for you to be going to all this trouble."

"You got it wrong, my friend."

"Do I? Are you saying that wasn't you out on the road tonight?"

"Out on *what* road? You're not making any sense."

"Somebody ran me down out there," Brody said. "And the last thing I saw was your car."

"What car? The unmarked? The patrol unit?"

Brody nodded.

"Come on, Carpenter, you know as well as I do that those units are standard-issue. They all look the same. So whoever mowed you down was either an imposter or one of our deputies gone rogue. But it sure as heck wasn't me."

"Why should I believe you?"

Frank shook his head in disgust. "I don't think you're in the position to be deciding who you should or shouldn't believe. The way I look at it, *you're* the one who set up Owen. And *you're* the one who knows where Anna and Adam are."

"You're out of your mind," Brody said. "Owen was my best friend. And you think I'd ever hurt Anna? You think I'd do anything to put my own son in danger?"

Frank was suddenly silent. Surprised.

"So she told you, did she?"

Brody nodded again. "I don't think she meant to, but yeah. And if you're crazy enough to believe I'd ever hurt either of them…"

"This isn't an act, is it?" Frank said. "You really *are* still in love with her."

"Is that a surprise?"

"No. No, I guess it isn't." He lowered the gun now. "And if it makes you feel any better, I'm sure she feels the same. It was always you, Brody. After you left she tried to convince herself that she was in love with me—doing it for Adam's sake—but it just didn't work for any of us."

Brody studied Frank's face. Saw the sincerity there.

This was, he realized, the first time the two of them had a conversation that wasn't filled with the heat of rivalry. One always trying to upstage the other.

Could Frank be telling the truth?

Were his hands clean in this?

Was he merely a cop, a concerned ex-husband who wanted to protect the woman he loved?

"So what now?" Brody asked, eyeing the weapon in Frank's hand. "If neither one of us is behind this, then who is? And where have they taken Anna and Adam?"

"What you said about that car on the road has me thinking. We were finally able to identify Santa Claus and his buddy. They were both registered with the department as CIs."

The sheriff's department often used confidential informants to help keep the deputies apprised of what was going on in the streets. All CIs were registered in a special database and paid through a fund set aside specifically for that purpose.

"So you weren't kidding about possible rogue deputies. Who were the CIs working for?"

"That's the problem," Frank said. "The records have been tampered with. We don't know who they were assigned to. My first instinct was that they must've been connected to *you* at one point, back when you were on the force, but I can see I was wrong. I let my own prejudice get in the way of my judgment."

"Join the club," Brody told him. It seemed they'd

both jumped to conclusions. "So we could be dealing with anyone. Anyone in the department."

Frank nodded and gestured. "Which makes calling all this in a very bad idea. Looks like we're on our own from here on—"

There was a crash down below.

The front door flying open.

Frank brought the gun up and turned, starting down the stairs, Brody right at his heels.

When they reached the bottom, to their complete surprise they found Anna stumbling to the sofa, soaked to the bone and out of breath, her eyes filled with panic and terror and tears.

"They've got Adam," she sobbed. "Oh, my sweet God, they've got Adam…"

Chapter Nineteen

Anna had never been so terrified in her life. Her chest constricted and she could barely breathe. She was wet and cold and miserable, but most of all worried. Worried that she'd never see her son and her mother again.

Brody and Frank moved to her.

"*Who* has Adam?" Frank asked. "Who took him?"

She shook her head. "I don't know, I don't know. There were two of them and they were wearing ski masks."

"Tell us exactly what happened."

Anna tried her best to tamp down her panic and catch her breath. But it wasn't working.

"I took a taxi home from Owen's place," she managed. "But when he dropped me off, I saw the deputy on the porch and the door hanging open, and before I could react, they came crashing past me, dragging Adam and Mom along with them. Then they shoved them in a car and took off."

"What did you do?" Brody asked. "Where have you been all this time?"

"I started running after them. Shouting at them to stop. Screaming for Adam. I don't know why the neighbors didn't report it. I must've looked like a crazy lady."

"Forget about the neighbors," Frank said. "They probably don't want to get involved."

"I kept running and running," Anna told them. "Even after I couldn't see the car anymore. I must've run a couple of miles. I don't know what I was thinking. I was out of my mind with panic."

Brody sat down next to her and pulled her into his arms. "Easy," he said. "Take it easy."

Anna welcomed his touch. Needed it. "They've got my son, Brody. *Our* son."

"I know," he said. "I know. We'll find him. We'll get him back."

"But how? We don't even know who they—"

The phone rang, cutting her off. The landline in the dining room. Mounted on the wall next to the kitchen doorway.

They all jerked their heads toward it, listening to its shrill ring pierce the air.

Frank started toward it, but Brody held a hand up, stopping him.

"Let Anna answer," he said. "It's gotta be them."

They all exchanged glances, and Anna knew she had no choice now but to overcome her panic and answer the phone. Adam's and Mom's lives might depend on it.

The phone continued to ring. She got to her feet, her legs trembling as she moved, a knot of dread burning in her stomach as she crossed to the dining room.

She got close to the receiver, stared at it, still trying to stifle her terror.

Then she picked it up.

"Hello?"

The voice on the other end was mechanical. Robotlike. The caller was using some kind of device to disguise it. "That was quite a display, Ms. Sanford. You should consider running a marathon."

"Who are you? Where's my son?"

"Sitting in his grandmother's arms as we speak. Cute kid you've got there."

"If you hurt them, I swear to God—"

"That's entirely up to you, now, isn't it?"

Anna tried to calm herself. "What do you want from me?"

"Come on, now, Anna, let's not play that game anymore. You know very well what we want."

"That stupid button," she spat. "The key that'll get you into Northboard."

"We know your brother gave it to you. He tried to double-cross us, back out on the whole plan. He even threatened to go to the sheriff. But we weren't about to let that happen."

"I don't believe you. You must have forced him into it. What did you threaten him with?"

The voice was silent a moment. Then: "The same thing we're using to threaten you, my dear. Your precious little Adam. And if you don't cooperate…"

Anna's panic rose again. "Don't hurt him—*please* don't hurt him."

"Then give us the button."

"But I don't *have* it. How can I give it to you if I don't know where…"

She stopped suddenly when she realized that Brody was standing next to her now, holding up a hand.

He had a disk between his fingers.

Anna knew he'd left the other disk with his friend Coffey, so this had to be a different one.

A new one.

Was it the *real* thing? Had he somehow managed to find it?

She spoke into the phone again. "All right," she said. "No games. Tell me what you want me to do."

"It's very simple," the voice said. "First, I want you to sit there for a while and think about what's at stake. If you think you're gonna get clever and call the police, try setting us up, you'll only be signing your son's death warrant. Grandma's, too."

Anna glanced at Brody then across at Frank.

"No police," she said. "I promise."

"Good, Anna. That's what I like to hear." He

paused. "Around about midnight, I want you to get into that car of yours and start driving."

"Where am I going?"

"There's a meatpacking plant on Mercer Street, the South Side, about a forty-minute drive from your house. You park just outside the front doors at twelve forty-five sharp and bring that button. We'll take it from there." He paused again. "You understand?"

"Yes, yes—and you'll have Adam and my mother with you?"

"As long as you cooperate."

"But how do I know you're telling the truth? How do I even know they're still alive?"

"That's easy enough to remedy."

Then there was a rustling sound and Mom's quavering voice came on the line: "Anna?"

"Mom—Mom—are you okay? Is Adam all right?"

"He's fine, dear. They haven't hurt us. They just want whatever it is Owen gave you and they promised they'll let us go."

Anna started to break down. "Mom... Oh, Mom..."

"Easy, hon. We'll be okay. Don't you worry, I won't let anything happen to Adam. He's safe with me."

Anna started to say something, but the rustling sound filled her ear again and the mechanical voice came back on the line.

"Twelve forty-five, Anna. Are we clear?"

Anna couldn't speak.

"Are. We. Clear?"

"Yes," Anna sobbed. "Yes. I'll be there. I'll be alone."

Without another word spoken, the line clicked.

"WE HAVE TO CALL THIS in," Frank said, pulling his cell phone from his pocket. "We should storm that place with every available man we've got."

"No!" Anna cried. "We can't take that chance. I promised him, *no police.*"

Frank ignored her and started to dial, but Brody crossed to him, grabbing his forearm.

"If you call it in, you'll tip our hand. You said yourself there may be rogue deputies involved in this thing."

"I was guessing about that. I could be wrong."

"And if you aren't?"

Frank thought about this then nodded. He pulled his arm away and dropped the phone back into his pocket. "All right, then. What's the plan?"

"I go in alone," Anna said. "Just like they told me. There's no other choice."

Brody shook his head. "That's not gonna happen."

"But you *heard* me on the phone. I promised him no police."

"I'm not a deputy anymore, remember? And Frank here's just an interested party at this point. And if you think either of us will let you go in there without some kind of backup, you're completely out of your mind."

"But you'll be risking Adam's life!"

"Listen to me, Anna. I guarantee you these people don't have any intention of letting any of you walk away from this thing alive. Adding me and Frank to the mix may be the only way to prevent you all from being killed."

Anna was torn. She knew Brody was talking sense, that the men they were dealing with were ruthless and cruel. But if anything went wrong, she'd never forgive herself.

"You have to trust me," Brody said. "I spent a year smuggling refugees out of one of the most dangerous places in the world. In all that time, I never lost a single life. Not one. And I don't intend to now."

"But he's my son."

"*Our* son. And they'll have to shoot me dead before I'll let anything happen to him."

"I'll double down on that," Frank said. "We've both got your back."

She looked from one to the other, saw the determination in their eyes. They were both good men, and she knew she was blessed to have them on her side. Any resentment she harbored toward either had vanished in the face of this nightmare.

"All right," she said softly. "How do we do this?"

"We've got a few hours before the rendezvous,"

Brody said then turned to Frank. "Are you familiar with this meatpacking plant?"

"I've never seen it, but I do know this. One of the CIs who attacked you two used to work for a place called American Beef. What do you bet we're talking about the same place?"

Brody nodded. "I'm sure it's no coincidence."

"Problem is, if they're a working meat plant, they're probably open night and day, which could be tricky."

Brody considered this then shook his head. "If they're keeping Adam and Sylvia there, I'm guessing the plant took a break for Christmas." He looked at Anna. "You have a laptop handy?"

"Sure, why?"

"I want to look at a satellite image of this place, see what we're dealing with."

"Smart thinking," Frank said. "I can hook us into the department's sat-com line."

Anna knew that at any other time it would have killed Frank to give Brody such a compliment, but they were past the pettiness now.

Brody looked out the window. "If this rain keeps up, we may be able to use it to our advantage. They won't see us coming."

"Except we don't know how many of them there are," Frank said. "That plant could be crawling with bad guys."

"They've already lost a couple of their men, and

they don't strike me as people who like to share. I figure two or three of them at the most."

"Which puts the odds at just about even. Let's hope you're right."

"Even if I'm not," Brody told him, "we've got another big advantage."

"Which is?"

"They don't know you're part of this. And they think I'm lying in a ditch on the side of the road."

Chapter Twenty

According to its internet profile, American Beef didn't deal directly with livestock but shipped in carcasses by the truckload for processing and packaging. Then another set of trucks transported those to some of the lesser grocery store chains throughout Cedarwood, Iowa, and its neighboring counties.

The plant had recently been the subject of a federal probe, after a disgruntled worker had taken video of what were believed to be unsafe food-handling practices. The video was deemed inconclusive evidence, however, and while the probe had turned up a few minor violations, the plant had been allowed to remain open for business.

The lot it stood on was dominated by a tall water tower that overlooked a seedy, rectangular brick building about the size of a small convalescent hospital. The adjacent parking structure was empty, and the loading dock was crowded with at least a half dozen idle trucks bearing the American Beef logo.

A tall, rusty chain-link fence topped by barbed

wire surrounded the place, and Anna had no idea what to expect as she pulled her car up to the gate.

There was no guard in the booth.

No lights shining in the building.

No sign of life anywhere.

Had they lied to her? Was this some kind of cruel joke being played on her for the amusement of sociopathic minds? Would she get inside and discover that Mom and Adam weren't even in there? Had *never* been in there?

No, she thought. *They're here.*

They have to be.

If they weren't, the creeps behind Owen's murder would never get what they wanted. They'd never take possession of this thing in her pocket that was so important to them.

Before she and Brody and Frank left the house, Brody had given her the button and told them where he'd found it. She had no idea why Owen had hidden it in that sheriff's car, but he must have had his reasons. Probably figured no one would ever think to look there.

And he was right. Brody had stumbled upon it only by pure luck. A small turn of fate that had worked in their favor.

The rain hammered her windshield, the wipers pumping hard but not doing a whole lot for visibility. Anna listened to that *thump…thump…thump…*and realized the sound was working in counterpoint to her rapidly beating heart.

She couldn't remember a time when she was so scared. Adam was her life, and if anything happened to him or Mom, if those monsters touched a hair on their heads…

She didn't want to think about that.

She couldn't allow herself to go down that cold, dark alleyway. It was too bleak down there.

Too heartbreaking.

Too…permanent.

Instead she sat there silently in the darkness, listening to the thumping wipers, the ceaseless rain, feeling the vibration of the car's idling engine as her gaze drifted to the digital clock on the dash.

It was 12:41 a.m.

Four minutes to go.

Just twelve hours ago she had been sitting in a house full of sheriff's deputies as they finished up their investigation of the break-in. The deputies had been there since very early in the morning, going over and over the chain of events, Frank and Joe Wilson making it clear to everyone that they thought Brody was behind it all.

They'd wanted to take him in for further questioning, but Brody had refused, and without any concrete evidence against him, they had finally given up and gone away. Just like that.

Anna had to admit that for just the briefest of

moments she had wondered about Brody. Frank's accusations against him had managed to work their way into her subconscious, planting the tiniest sliver of doubt in her mind.

But she dismissed that doubt the moment it surfaced.

As angry as she might have been at Brody, as hurt as she was by the things he had done to her in the past, Anna had known—and *still* knew—that the father of her child, the best friend her brother had ever had, the man she had loved since she was sixteen years old, would never betray her like that.

Brody Carpenter was not a killer.

Brody Carpenter had never cared enough about money to enable him to do the kinds of things that these men were willing to do.

His time in Darfur and Chad had more than proved that. He hadn't been there as a mercenary, as someone sent into the country to exploit and abuse for profit or political gain.

He had gone there as a savior. A protector.

And that's why he had come back to Cedarwood. That's why he had answered Owen's call without hesitation. To do what he had been trained to do, selflessly and without compromise.

Trouble. Too late for me.

Protect Anna.

He hadn't asked for forgiveness. He hadn't even

expected it from her. All he had wanted was to explain, to apologize, to try to make her understand what he had been going through all those years ago when he walked out the door.

He'd made it clear that his behavior had been inexcusable and that he was sorry for what he had done to her. And when he had come to her last night and laid her across the bed, she took him with a hunger she hadn't known she possessed.

Yet she'd been conflicted about having him in her life again. She was afraid to completely let herself go, to once again fall under that intoxicating spell of his, because she feared that once his work was done, he might not stick around.

She had carefully weighed whether to tell him about Adam and had been unable to do it. She hadn't wanted to keep him in Cedarwood that way. Hadn't wanted him to feel obligated to stick around.

Now, as she sat there watching the clock, counting off the seconds, she realized just how silly she'd been. If they all managed to get through this terrifying night in one piece, she would welcome Brody back into her life with open arms.

And she would forgive him. Just as her father would have. Just as her mother had.

Without forgiveness, there is no future.

And Anna knew, with great certainty, that was exactly what she wanted with Brody.

A future.

WHEN THE CLOCK ON THE dash ticked over to 12:43, Brody said, "Two minutes. We'd better get moving."

He was crouched low on the seat next to Anna, looking out through the rain toward the packing plant, his jaw set, his gaze unwavering. He was in work mode, all business, and if Anna had to rely on someone to save Adam, she knew there was no one better or more determined than Brody.

Frank was in the backseat. "I'll go in first," he said. "I'll take the left flank, you take the right. You ready, Anna?"

"Yes."

"Let's do it, then."

Bracing herself, Anna popped open her door. Using an umbrella for protection against the rain, she climbed out of the car and walked ten steps to the packing plant's gate.

Her legs were trembling, her nerves doing somersaults in her stomach.

There was no lock on the gate. Just a wooden handle. She grasped it and rolled it aside, leaving enough room for her car to fit through, then walked back and climbed behind the wheel.

Putting the car in gear, she followed the plan Brody and Frank had laid out for them in her living room and slowly pulled through the gate.

The moment she was past it, Frank cracked his

door open and rolled out, disappearing into the darkness.

A few seconds later, Brody leaned toward her, touching her forearm.

"Remember to play your part," he said. "You're alone, you're scared and you just want to get this thing over with."

"I won't have to do much acting."

He nodded then pulled a pistol from his waistband. "I took this from your closet. If I don't come out of this thing alive, I—"

"Don't talk like that."

"We both know it's a possibility. If anything happens to me in there, I want you to use this thing. Do whatever you have to do to get your mother and Adam out of that place."

He handed her the gun. "Keep it in your waistband, at the small of your back." He started to go, then hesitated. Turned to her. "I know I've said this before—but I love you, Anna. More than anyone should ever be allowed to love someone. And I'm sorry for all the pain I put you through."

Then he squeezed her arm, cracked open his door and slipped away, disappearing into the rain.

Chapter Twenty-One

The rain didn't let up, which was both a blessing and a curse.

Brody crouched under the water tower, his gaze on the packing plant, but getting there had taken some time and he was soaked through. Hair, shoes, pants, shirt—every part of him was dripping water, and the chill in the air wasn't helping much.

Even the gun Frank loaned him was soaked. That didn't mean it wouldn't fire, but handling it wouldn't be as easy with it wet.

The plan they'd formulated was a simple one.

Maybe too simple.

But with only satellite footage available, and no blueprints or floor plans to guide them, they'd known that their best option was a quick and dirty stealth assault:

—Make entry;

—Take out anyone who got in their way;

—Find Adam and Sylvia.

Despite their differences, Brody had always

thought of Frank as a man who could handle himself, and he knew that the training offered by the Cedarwood Sheriff's Department was some of the best in the country. Frank was no stranger to tactical maneuvers and was bound to be an asset here.

But if the men inside that plant were rogue deputies, as Frank suspected, then they would've gone through the very same training.

And that could be a problem.

This wasn't the first time Brody had been in a situation like this. The geography had been different, and the target had been a Janjaweed compound in the middle of nowhere, but he and another man had managed to silently put down ten guards before freeing a cell full of African farm women—the compound's personal sex slaves.

He had come very close to losing his life that night, and he knew that if he miscalculated this time, if there were more people involved in this thing than his instincts told him there were…he might not walk away.

But that didn't matter as long as Adam and Sylvia were safe.

Nothing else mattered.

He kept his gaze on the building. There were no lights inside. No signs of life whatsoever. He was directly across from the loading dock, several big rigs and small refrigerator trucks sitting silently in the surrounding darkness. He knew they'd make good cover as he worked his way toward the building.

He had no idea what time it was, but he figured no more than two minutes had passed since he'd left Anna near the gate.

She would be driving forward now, rolling up close to the front doors and waiting for someone to make contact.

He knew she was afraid. He had seen the fear in her eyes as he told her he loved her. He didn't like leaving her out there on her own, but what choice did he have? She was a strong woman, and if things went sour for him tonight, she'd do whatever it took to get their son back.

A few hours ago he had been overjoyed to hear the news about Adam. But now that joy was tempered by worry and fear, feelings he'd have to fight off if he was going to be effective here.

Just think of it as another mission, Brody. Visualize Darfur and do what you have to do.

Shoving aside all emotion, he got to his feet, checked the building one last time for any sign of movement then darted across the lot to the first truck parked near the loading dock.

Crouching low, he slipped under the container and waited near the left rear tire, all the while keeping his gaze on the building.

Still no movement.

Now that he was closer, however, he thought he

saw light in one of the windows. A faint yellow glow that was barely visible through the falling rain.

He needed an even closer look.

Steeling himself, he got to his feet and made another quick dash, hiding behind one of the refrigerator trucks. Moving from truck to truck, he made his way to the loading-dock steps and waited there a moment, staying low behind the dock's cement ledge.

There was definitely light in that window.

After a quick scan of the area, he moved up onto the dock and stood under the overhang, thankful to be out of the rain. Flattening against the rollaway door, he moved sideways to the window, stopping just short of it.

Crouching again, he got below the windowsill and carefully peeked in.

The room inside was dark, but beyond this, through an open doorway, was a narrow corridor that led to another doorway.

This was where the light was coming from.

It was hard to tell with the constant drumming of the rain, but he thought he heard voices coming from in there.

He glanced around, looking for a way inside. There was a door to his far right of the loading dock, protected by a dead bolt. He moved to check it and wasn't surprised to find it locked.

Fortunately, he'd never had much problem with

locks. Pulling out his wallet, he removed the paper clip he kept in one of its pockets then unfolded the clip and straightened one end.

Gripping the other end between his forefinger and thumb, he inserted the length of wire into the narrow part of the keyhole, carefully lined up the tumblers then pushed it deep and worked it around inside.

It took some effort, but the lock finally gave and the dead bolt turned.

A moment later he was inside the packing plant, dripping rainwater on the scarred linoleum floor. There was a corridor ahead of him, and now that the rain was muffled by the door, he could definitely hear voices. They were indistinct from this distance, but he knew what direction they were coming from.

Pulling the gun out from under his shirt, he headed toward them.

As he reached the end of the corridor, he waited, listening for footsteps. Heard none.

Shifting to his left, he raised the gun and ducked low as he pivoted into the adjoining corridor, ready to squeeze off a shot.

The corridor was empty. There were deep shadows at the far end but no movement there.

The doorway with the light was located on the right side. He rose to his full height and moved against the wall, keeping the gun ready, working his way toward that room.

He could hear the voices clearly now but realized

that there was a tinny quality to them, as if they were coming from a speaker.

Reaching the doorway, he chanced a quick look inside and saw a break room with an old tube television set tucked into one corner, tuned to a classic movie channel.

In other words, a bust.

He was about to duck away when a whisper came out of the darkness behind him.

"Glad you could make it, scooter boy."

Brody whirled.

A man wearing a ski mask emerged from the darkness at the far end of the hall, pointing a small assault rifle at Brody. The kind the local drug dealers used. He was one of the men Brody had confronted in Anna's house—the guy he'd stopped on the stairs.

"Put the gun on the floor," the man whispered.

Brody looked at the pistol in his hand then leaned down and placed it on the linoleum.

The man stepped toward him now and Brody didn't hesitate. He plunged forward, tackling the guy, grabbing his gun arm. Wrapping both hands around the wrist, Brody squeezed hard as the man hammered at him with his free hand, trying to break him loose.

The fingers slackened and the gun clattered to the floor, and they went down hard, Brody struggling to gain control. He grabbed blindly at the man, getting hold of a handful of fleece, yanking the ski mask off his head. As they rolled into the light from the doorway, Brody got a look at the man's face and was surprised by what he saw.

It was Joe Wilson.

Frank's partner.

Wilson scowled at him and brought a knee up into Brody's stomach, knocking the wind out of him. As Brody clutched himself and rolled away, gasping for breath, Wilson got to his feet, frantically shuffled around then disappeared from view.

When he came back into the light, he was once again carrying his assault rifle, a self-satisfied grin on his face.

He pointed the muzzle at Brody. "I guess you aren't such a hotshot after all, are you, Carpen—"

A silencer *plocked*. Three holes opened up in Wilson's chest, the impact knocking him back into the darkness, his rifle skidding across the floor.

Pulling himself upright, Brody staggered to his feet and turned to find Frank Matson, dripping wet, standing at the opposite end of the corridor.

"Just goes to show you can't trust anyone these days," Frank said.

Then he pointed his silencer at Brody.

"Including me."

Chapter Twenty-Two

It was 12:49.

Still no sign of life in the building.

Anna was parked in front of American Beef's entrance, worried that something had gone wrong, wondering why her son's kidnappers hadn't yet come outside.

Were they waiting for her to make the first move?

Should she get out of the car and see if the front doors were locked?

Five more minutes, she thought. *Five more minutes, then you go inside.*

She glanced at the pistol on the seat beside her. Scooping it up, she ejected the magazine, checked to make sure it was full of cartridges then snapped it back into place.

She didn't really know what she was doing. She had no use for guns and still wasn't quite sure she could actually pull the trigger. If it came down to the bad guys versus her family, she'd have to find a way to get past the uncertainty, point at the target and squeeze.

12:50.

The longest minute of her life, and still nothing.

Pulling the pistol into her lap now, she closed her eyes and sent up a prayer.

Help me, Lord. Help me.

BRODY COULDN'T QUITE believe what he was seeing. "What are you doing, Frank?"

"Come on, Carpenter. You're smarter than that. I'm surprised you didn't already figure it out on your own." He smiled. "I'm afraid I lied to you earlier. I *am* the guy who mowed you down on the road, and I gotta tell you, it felt pretty good."

"You think you're actually gonna get away with this?"

Matson laughed. "It took some improvising, but it looks like I already have."

"What does that mean?"

"Turns out I was right about you all along. After I shoot you—in self-defense, of course—there's gonna be an investigation. And guess what they'll find when they open up Wilson's private email?"

"No idea," Brody said.

"Enough evidence to prove that you and h in cahoots all along. That you colluded with W s confidential informants to try and get that button from Anna. But the button I give them will be a blank, so nobody'll be quite sure what the fuss was all about."

"You're insane. What could Northboard have that's worth all this killing?"

"My ex-brother-in-law told me there are a number of things in that building that could catch a pretty penny. But what I'm looking to grab are the plans for a brand-new weapon they're developing. I've already got buyers starting to line up. And these people have deep, deep pockets."

"Even with a key card," Brody said, "you think you can just walk in there and take whatever you want?"

"That's the beauty of having an inside man. Owen told me that every Christmas Eve, Northboard throws its office party—a big old shindig—and everyone in the building is invited. Including most of the security staff. I figure that's the perfect time to slip inside and do what needs to be done."

"You're dreaming," Brody told him.

"Maybe so," Frank said, "but a man's gotta dream. The way I see it, when this is over, I'm the hero and I get the girl. Just like last time."

Brody frowned. "Last time?"

"Who do you think set you up for the fall four years ago? Made it look like you took that bribe?"

Brody felt his chest tighten. His eyes must have shown his anger.

"That's right, Carpenter. I didn't expect you to be acquitted, but it all worked out in the end. You left town and I got Anna." He smiled. "But this time out, I won't be making the same mistakes. And I don't have to worry about you coming back."

"What about Adam?" Brody asked. "Where is he?"

"He's safe. Always has been. We never made much of a connection, but I wouldn't dream of hurting that boy. He and Sylvia were just an excuse to get you out here." He paused. "And when all is said and done, Anna's gonna be telling that boy that his daddy was one of the cruelest human beings ever to walk this good green earth. Assuming she tells him you're related at all."

Brody clinched his teeth. "You really are insane."

"What I am is in love," Frank said. "But I guess that pretty much amounts to the same thing."

He smiled again and Brody sensed that this was his cue. His gaze zeroed in on Frank's trigger finger and when he saw the flicker of movement there—

—he dove sideways.

The silencer coughed, two shots in rapid succession, both of them whizzing past Brody's head as he rolled into the darkness and scrambled to his feet.

Then a third shot came, catching him in the shoulder, and he nearly went down again, intense heat ripping through him. Pushing past the pain, he ran toward the far end of the hallway, found another doorway there and slipped inside.

He heard Frank cursing behind him, his footsteps echoing against the corridor walls. Picking up speed, Brody crossed through what looked like a packaging room and raced past a wide conveyor belt, heading toward a lighted doorway at the far end.

When he went through that doorway, the temperature dropped about sixty degrees. He was inside a massive refrigerator, surrounded by hanging carcasses of beef.

ANNA LOOKED AT THE clock on the dash.

1:00 a.m.

She had waited a lot longer than she'd intended, nervous about making a move, but now she grabbed the pistol from her lap and shoved it into her waistband at the small of her back, just as Brody had instructed.

Snatching up her umbrella, she threw the car door open and climbed out, shielding herself from the rain.

She stared at the building's entrance, hoping that her movements might have alerted someone inside. But she saw nothing but blackness beyond the glass doors, and no one came out to greet her.

She wondered about Brody and Frank.

Had they been successful?

Was that why no one was coming outside?

If so, then why hadn't they told her? Why hadn't one of them come to get her, to assure her that the bad guys had been caught and that Adam and Mom were safe?

Anna approached the entrance, moving onto a short covered walkway. Setting her umbrella on the asphalt, she moved up to the doors and put her face against the glass, peering into the room beyond.

All she saw was a rundown lobby area, bathed in shadow and moonlight. There was a reception desk and several framed posters of assorted meats hung on the wall behind it, surrounding the American Beef logo.

She tried the door, found it unlocked.

Should she go inside?

Part of her wanted to turn and flee, but she knew she really had no choice.

If anything happens to me, Brody had said, *do whatever you have to do to get your mother and Adam out of that place.*

Mustering up her courage, Anna pulled the door open and stepped into the darkness. She was only a few feet inside when she decided to throw caution to the wind.

"Hello?" she called. "Is anyone here?"

No response.

She moved deeper into the lobby, her gaze shifting to a hallway just beyond the reception desk.

"Hello? This is Anna Sanford, is anyone around?"

And that's when she heard it: a muffled cry. Someone calling for help.

Mom?

Pulling the gun from the small of her back, Anna sucked in a breath, swept past the reception desk and headed down that hallway.

Chapter Twenty-Three

Brody's shoulder was leaking.

Thanks to the refrigerated air, the initial pain had subsided somewhat, giving way to numbness, but he knew that eventually that would wear off and the pain would return full force.

For the moment, however, he could deal with it.

The problem was the blood.

Frank's shot had gone straight through his shoulder, which was leaking profusely. He was trailing blood behind him—a trail that would be hard to miss in this lighted room. He knew he'd made a mistake coming in here.

He clamped a hand to his shoulder, trying to control the flow, but it wasn't doing him much good. Worse yet, he was starting to weaken from the loss of all that fluid.

He had no idea where Frank was at this point, and being weaponless didn't give him great comfort. He stood behind the carcass of a fairly large steer, one of at least a hundred that hung from meat hooks in this massive room.

He kept his gaze on the doorway, knowing that sooner or later, Frank would walk through it.

It didn't take long for his prediction to come true.

Frank was carrying Wilson's assault rifle now, keeping it tucked close to his body.

"I know you're in here, Carpenter. You're leaking oil like a rusty old Buick." His gaze went to the floor, scanning it for signs of blood. "We both know how this is gonna end, so you might as well come out and get it over with."

Brody didn't move.

"I can't wait to see the look on Anna's face when she realizes you betrayed her again." He laughed. "And the sex. Can't wait for that, either. Comfort sex is the best, isn't it? Especially when you've got a woman like Anna in your bed."

Brody knew that Frank was trying get a reaction out of him. Keeping his hand clamped on his shoulder, he stepped backward, crossing to the protection of another carcass. He glanced at the floor and didn't see blood this time.

"Woman really knows how to please a man, wouldn't you say? We had us a whole lot of fun after you ran away, and she took me places I've never been before."

He was working his way toward Brody, following

that trail of blood. Brody stepped sideways now, moving on to yet another carcass.

"There's no question she'll be devastated after tonight," Frank said. "But I'm at my best when a woman is vulnerable. And don't you worry. I'll make her forget about you this time."

ANNA FLEW DOWN THE hallway.

"Mom?" she shouted. "Is that you?"

She heard the muffled cries again and turned a corner, spotting a closed door at the end of another short hallway. The sounds came from behind it.

She rushed to the door, tried the knob, found it locked. Pounded her fists on the wood.

"Mom? Are you in there? Is Adam with you?"

More muffled cries. She couldn't make them out, but she recognized her mother's voice.

Stepping back, she brought a foot up high and kicked at the door, right near the knob. It buckled but didn't crack.

She tried again, and then again, and the wood finally began to splinter. After she gave it three more solid kicks, the door finally broke loose and swung open.

Mom and Adam were bound and gagged, tied to a chair. Both of them were wearing blindfolds.

Anna rushed to them, ripping at the bonds, pulling away the blindfolds, and when she had them free, she grabbed Adam and hugged him with everything she had.

"Oh my God, baby, are you all right?"

Adam was crying now. She could tell that he was terrified. But he nodded in answer to her question. "I'm okay, Mommy."

She turned to her mother. "What about you?"

"I'm a little shook up," Sylvia said. "But I'm fine. Is Brody with you?"

Anna nodded. "Frank, too. They're somewhere inside. But I need to get you two out of here. Get you to my car."

Sylvia returned the nod and they headed out the door.

MATSON HAD FINALLY stopped talking. Probably figured he'd get the job done easier if he wasn't constantly telegraphing his position.

The good news: Brody was still alive.

The bad news: he was losing energy fast, and he had no idea where in this sea of beef Frank might be.

He found out soon enough.

Deciding it was time to move again, he circled backward and crossed toward another slab of beef. But the moment he reached it, it suddenly exploded, a hail of bullets shredding it to pieces.

Narrowly missing being hit, Brody dove to safety, scrambling to a corner of the room. He crouched there, renewing his grip on his shoulder, his strength draining with every breath he took.

As he looked at the floor again, he realized he'd left another trail of blood. And just beyond the row of carcasses in front of him, was Frank—

—headed in his direction.

ANNA WAS HUSTLING MOM and Adam into the front seat when she heard the gunshots.

She jerked her head toward the building.

Brody and Frank. One of them was in trouble. Maybe both.

"Lock yourself in," she said to Sylvia. "And if I'm not back here in five minutes, get Adam out of here and call the sheriff."

Sylvia looked stricken. "What are you going to do?"

Anna pulled the pistol from her waistband again. "Whatever I have to."

"I'VE GOTTA ADMIT I'M a little disappointed, Carpenter." Frank was moving toward Brody, the assault rifle aimed at his chest. "I was expecting a little more fight out of you."

Brody was trapped in the corner. Every syllable he uttered was an effort for him. "She'll never...believe you, Frank."

"Oh, she'll believe me. I'm pretty convincing when I'm motivated."

"The only thing motivating you...is money."

"What—you don't think I'm capable of loving someone?"

"You're a sociopath," Brody said, feeling his adrenaline rise. "You don't even know what love is. Owen used to be your brother-in-law. He meant everything to the woman you claim to care about, but did you feel anything when you shot him?"

Matson shrugged. "I was a little annoyed he wouldn't tell me what I wanted to know."

"That just proves my point. You're incapable of emotion. And I'm betting that's why Anna divorced you. She could see right through the facade. Imagine what'll happen when she takes a deeper look and sees your black heart."

Matson frowned at him now. "You got a lot to say for a dead man." His eyes narrowed. "I think it's time we got this over with. Your buddy Owen is waiting for you in the after—"

"Frank?"

Matson flinched and took a step backward. Anna stood at the far end of the row of carcasses, staring at Frank in disbelief.

Frank did his best to cover, gesturing to Brody. "It's him, babe. He's the one who set this all up. He tried to jump me in the hallway."

Anna wasn't buying it. It was obvious by her expression that she'd heard more than enough to know that he was lying. She brought the pistol up and pointed it at him.

"I can't believe you killed Owen." She shoved her free hand into her pocket, pulled out the security tag Brody had given her. She held it up. "And for this? This is worth that much to you?"

"I did it for us, babe. You and me. Owen could've had part of it, too, but he got stupid."

"So you shot him."

"We're gonna be rich, Anna. Don't you get that? You won't have to slog in that shop every day, trying to get ahead. We can do whatever we want. Go wherever we want to."

Anna's face hardened. "I wouldn't cross the street with you," she told him then dropped the RFID tag to the floor and raised her foot over it. "And you can kiss that money goodbye."

As she brought the foot down, Frank's face filled with panic.

"No!" he shouted and swung the assault rifle toward her, fingering the trigger.

In the split second before Frank fired, Brody used every last ounce of strength he had and sprang from the corner, grabbing Frank's legs.

They went down hard and the assault rifle chattered wildly, sending bullets into the air. Then Brody was on top of him, pummeling Frank's face, his chest, hammering him over and over again, channeling his rage into the effort, until Frank was out cold.

Then Brody staggered to his feet, and Anna rushed to him, pulling him into her arms, hugging him, kissing him, murmuring in his ear.

"I love you, Brody. I'll always love you. And I forgive you for everything. Everything."

Pain shot through Brody's shoulder, and he knew he was leaking blood all over her. But he didn't care.

He was back in the arms of the woman he loved.

And that was all that mattered.

Chapter Twenty-Four

Frank Matson refused to confess to his crimes, but it didn't make a difference. It turned out that Joe Wilson had survived the gunshots in the hallway and was all too happy to cooperate in exchange for a chance at parole.

Frank, however, would never get that chance. The D.A. was predicting multiple life sentences, and nobody involved in the case wanted to take odds against her.

On Christmas Eve, Anna found herself caught in the whirlwind of the investigation, answering questions, looking at photographs. She'd been asked to identify the two men in the van—all part of the evidence against Frank—and she'd had no trouble picking them out of a photo array.

Brody spent Christmas Eve, and several days after, in the hospital, getting his wounds stitched up and telling his version of events.

A lot of the sheriff's office brass came to see him,

and one of them even mentioned the possibility of Brody going back to his old job.

"You got a lousy deal, Carpenter. Maybe we can make up for that. Put you where you belong—on the homicide squad."

Brody didn't make any commitments. He told Anna that he wasn't sure he wanted to go back to the department, and she didn't really blame him.

Too much history there. For both of them.

She didn't care what he did with his life, as long as he stayed with her here in Cedarwood and got to know his son.

Adam had come through this trauma like a champ. He hadn't even complained when Anna told him they were going to delay Christmas a bit, waiting for Brody to get out of the hospital. She hadn't told him that Brody was his father, yet. Figured that was too much, too soon.

But the time would come, and she knew that Adam would be thrilled by the news.

THEY CELEBRATED Christmas on New Year's Day.

This seemed appropriate to Anna. The beginning of a new year and a new life. They all still had an empty spot in their hearts for Owen, but they knew he was with them in spirit and always would be.

As they sat by the tree, exchanging gifts—Mom, Adam, Brody and Anna—Brody, still wearing a sling, handed a box to Adam, the wrapping paper covered with multicolored dinosaurs.

"Is this mine?" Adam asked.

"Sure is," Brody said then tousled his son's head. "A little something to make up for breaking the wheels on your sheriff's car."

Adam grinned, unceremoniously ripping the wrapping paper free. When he got the box open, he paused and sucked in a breath, his eyes going wide with surprise and excitement.

Then he dove in, pulling out a toy motorcycle.

A black Harley-Davidson.

Anna's heart filled with joy as she watched him pull the motorcycle to his chest then jump into Brody's arms, giving him a thankful hug.

She knew that everything would be all right from here on out. That the fantasy she'd had so many years ago was finally coming true.

* * * * *

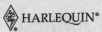

HARLEQUIN®

INTRIGUE®

COMING NEXT MONTH

Available December 7, 2010

REQUEST YOUR FREE BOOKS!

2 FREE NOVELS PLUS 2 FREE GIFTS!

 HARLEQUIN®

INTRIGUE®

Breathtaking Romantic Suspense

YES! Please send me 2 FREE Harlequin Intrigue® novels and my 2 FREE gifts (gifts are worth about $10). After receiving them, if I don't wish to receive any more books, I can return the shipping statement marked "cancel." If I don't cancel, I will receive 6 brand-new novels every month and be billed just $4.24 per book in the U.S. or $4.99 per book in Canada. That's a saving of at least 15% off the cover price! It's quite a bargain! Shipping and handling is just 50¢ per book.* I understand that accepting the 2 free books and gifts places me under no obligation to buy anything. I can always return a shipment and cancel at any time. Even if I never buy another book from Harlequin, the two free books and gifts are mine to keep forever.

182/382 HDN E5MG

Name _____ (PLEASE PRINT)

Address _____ Apt. #

City _____ State/Prov. _____ Zip/Postal Code

Signature (if under 18, a parent or guardian must sign)

Mail to the **Harlequin Reader Service:**
IN U.S.A.: P.O. Box 1867, Buffalo, NY 14240-1867
IN CANADA: P.O. Box 609, Fort Erie, Ontario L2A 5X3

Not valid for current subscribers to Harlequin Intrigue books.

**Are you a subscriber to Harlequin Intrigue books and
want to receive the larger-print edition? Call 1-800-873-8635 today!**

* Terms and prices subject to change without notice. Prices do not include applicable taxes. N.Y. residents add applicable sales tax. Canadian residents will be charged applicable provincial taxes and GST. Offer not valid in Quebec. This offer is limited to one order per household. All orders subject to approval. Credit or debit balances in a customer's account(s) may be offset by any other outstanding balance owed by or to the customer. Please allow 4 to 6 weeks for delivery. Offer available while quantities last.

Your Privacy: Harlequin is committed to protecting your privacy. Our Privacy Policy is available online at www.eHarlequin.com or upon request from the Reader Service. From time to time we make our lists of customers available to reputable third parties who may have a product or service of interest to you. If you would prefer we not share your name and address, please check here. ☐

Help us get it right—We strive for accurate, respectful and relevant communications. To clarify or modify your communication preferences, visit us at www.ReaderService.com/consumerchoice.

HI10R

HARLEQUIN®

A Romance

FOR EVERY MOOD™

Spotlight on
Classic

Quintessential, modern love stories
that are romance at its finest.

See the next page
to enjoy a sneak peek from
the Harlequin® Romance series.

CATCLASSHR10

See below for a sneak peek from our classic Harlequin® Romance® line.

Introducing DADDY BY CHRISTMAS by Patricia Thayer.

MIA caught sight of Jarrett when he walked into the open lobby. It was hard not to notice the man. In a charcoal business suit with a crisp white shirt and striped tie covered by a dark trench coat, he looked more Wall Street than small-town Colorado.

Mia couldn't blame him for keeping his distance. He was probably tired of taking care of her.

Besides, why would a man like Jarrett McKane be interested in her? Why would he want to take on a woman expecting a baby? Yet he'd done so many things for her. He'd been there when she'd needed him most. How could she not care about a man like that?

Heart pounding in her ears, she walked up behind him. Jarrett turned to face her. "Did you get enough sleep last night?"

"Yes, thanks to you," she said, wondering if he'd thought about their kiss. Her gaze went to his mouth, then she quickly glanced away. "And thank you for not bringing up my meltdown."

Jarrett couldn't stop looking at Mia. Blue was definitely her color, bringing out the richness of her eyes.

"What meltdown?" he said, trying hard to focus on what she was saying. "You were just exhausted from lack of sleep and worried about your baby."

He couldn't help remembering how, during the night, he'd kept going in to watch her sleep. How strange was that? "I hope you got enough rest."

She nodded. "Plenty. And you're a good neighbor for

HREXP1210

coming to my rescue."

He tensed. Neighbor? *What neighbor kisses you like I did?* "That's me, just the full-service landlord," he said, trying to keep the sarcasm out of his voice. He started to leave, but she put her hand on his arm.

"Jarrett, what I meant was you went beyond helping me." Her eyes searched his face. "I've asked far too much of you."

"Did you hear me complain?"

She shook her head. "You should. I feel like I've taken advantage."

"Like I said, I haven't minded."

"And I'm grateful for everything…"

Grasping her hand on his arm, Jarrett leaned forward. The memory of last night's kiss had him aching for another. "I didn't do it for your gratitude, Mia."

Gorgeous tycoon Jarrett McKane has never believed in Christmas—but he can't help being drawn to soon-to-be-mom Mia Saunders! Christmases past were spent alone…and now Jarrett may just have a fairy-tale ending for all his Christmases future!

*Available December 2010,
only from Harlequin® Romance®.*

HREXP1210

MYSTERY CASE FILES

**ENJOY ALL FOUR INSTALLMENTS
OF THIS NEW AND INTRIGUING**

BLACKPOOL MYSTERY

SERIES!

Follow an American couple,
two amateur detectives who are keen
to pursue clever killers who think they
have gotten away with everything!

Stolen
Jordan Gray
Available August 2010

Vanished
Jordan Gray
Available November 2010

Submerged
Jordan Gray
Available February 2011

Unearthed
Jordan Gray
Available May 2011

**BASED ON THE BESTSELLING
RAVENHEARST GAME
FROM BIG FISH GAMES!**

BIG FISH Games™

www.mysterycasefiles.com

MCF0810R